THE FRONT:
RED DEVILS

ALSO BY DAVID MOODY

THE HATER SERIES
HATER
DOG BLOOD
THEM OR US

THE AUTUMN SERIES
AUTUMN
AUTUMN: THE CITY
AUTUMN: PURIFICATION
AUTUMN: DISINTEGRATION
AUTUMN: AFTERMATH
AUTUMN: THE HUMAN CONDITION

STRANGERS
STRAIGHT TO YOU
TRUST

ALSO IN THIS SERIES

THE FRONT: SCREAMING EAGLES
by Timothy W. Long

THE FRONT: BERLIN OR BUST
coming soon from Craig DiLouie

THE FRONT: RED DEVILS

by David Moody
with
Craig DiLouie and Timothy W. Long

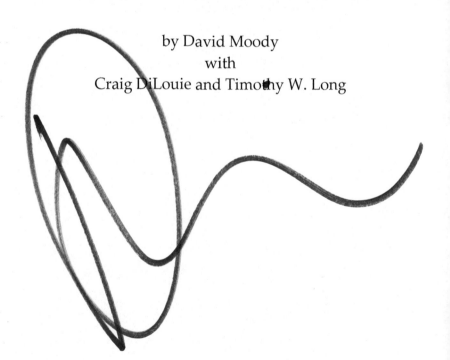

The right of David Moody to be identified as the author
of this work has been asserted by him in accordance with
the Copyright, Designs and Patents Act 1988.

This is a work of fiction. All of the characters,
organisations and events portrayed in this novel are
either products of the author's imagination
or are used fictitiously.

First published in 2017 by Infected Books

ISBN: 978-0-9576563-6-9

A CIP catalogue record for this book
is available from the British Library

Cover Designed by Eloise J. Knapp
www.ekcoverdesign.com

Edited by Wayne Simmons

www.davidmoody.net

www.infectedbooks.co.uk

POLONEZKÖY CAMP, ŁOBROWA, POLAND
SEPTEMBER 1944

SS-Obergruppenführer Jakob Wolfensohn marched along the narrow corridor towards the dead heart of the extermination camp, his entourage following nervously in his wake, chasing after the tails of his leather greatcoat. SS-Unterscharführer Ruprecht Weigle's heart raced as he brought up the rear. The noise of marching jackboots was deafening, amplified out of all proportion by the close confines of the grey stone castle walls. Weigle's nervousness was such that he thought he might pass out, but he didn't dare. He could not picture a more intimidating place to be, nor a more intimidating commander to be escorting.

Weigle was not alone in his unease. This cold, oppressive, hate and death-fuelled place instilled fear in even the blackest Nazi heart. Wolfensohn's aggression and clinical hostility was renowned throughout the Reich, and yet even his pulse quickened as they neared the experimentation room.

They were all waiting for him, as ordered. Wolfensohn could see the nervousness in their faces; the way their eyes followed his every move, and how they almost competed with each other to be the first to salute and *'Seig Heil!'*. He strode to the front of the room and sat in an empty chair, facing the wall. The grey concrete was pockmarked. Blood stains and splatters. There were tide marks on the floor.

Obersturmbannführer Scherler, chief of the camp and an odious little wretch in Wolfensohn's opinion, sat down beside him. 'I think you will be pleased by our progress, Herr Obergruppenführer,' he said.

'I hope for your sake you are right, Scherler. The Führer grows tired of your excuses.'

Scherler squirmed, his mouth dry. He knew what was at stake here, and he also knew he was running out of chances. He was relieved when an inconspicuous-looking door opened and Untersturmführer Honigsman entered and saluted. Behind Honigsman, two civilian scientists followed. After them were two stormtroopers, one of whom dragged a prisoner behind him: a pitifully weak-looking man with a hollowed-out chest, patchy hair, and limbs which looked like skin-wrapped bones, devoid of all muscle and strength. Wolfensohn regarded the prisoner with a mix of curiosity and disdain. His disdain extended to the scientists also. 'I have little time for these people. It's soldiers like us who will win this war, not ineffective underlings such as this.'

One of the scientists approached. The taller of the two, this was Professor Anton Eisen, a biologist from Berlin. 'With respect, Herr Obergruppenführer, the serum we have developed will make your soldiers more powerful than you could imagine. We will—'

'Quiet!' Scherler bellowed, jumping to his feet. 'You will not address the Obergruppenführer directly. Is that understood?'

Professor Eisen nodded meekly and backed away.

The stormtroopers shackled the prisoner to the wall, though the man had such little fight remaining that any one of the Nazis would have easily been able to deal with him on their own. He made no attempt to resist, all energy gone. His fate had been sealed the moment he'd arrived at Polonezköy, he'd known it all along. It wasn't a matter of *if* he died here, it was a question of *when*. He looked at the boots of the Nazis watching him – not daring to look directly into their faces – and hoped it would be soon.

Wolfensohn was growing impatient. The two scientists were busying themselves around a rickety wooden table with no apparent sense of urgency. '*Schnell!*' he yelled, filling the room with noise. 'My time is being wasted here.'

Professor Eisen looked at Obersturmbannführer Scherler for permission to begin. Scherler nodded, and Eisen cleared his throat. 'With apologies. We are ready now.'

Eisen may have been ready, but his colleague clearly wasn't. He continued preparing phials and syringes.

Eisen cleared his throat. 'Doctor Månsson, it is time.'

Månsson looked up, but would not be hurried. 'This process requires great care. If the agent was to be let loose in this confined space, we would all bare witness to its incredible power first-hand.'

'Show me your research now, Doctor Månsson, or it is my power you will see first hand,' Wolfensohn warned. 'I'll warrant that whatever you have in your damn test tubes is no match for me.'

Månsson almost took the bait, but resisted. Like the prisoner of war shackled to the wall next to him, he too knew his fate was sealed. Yet Månsson had no desire to die just yet.

Wolfensohn turned to Scherler again. 'Is the involvement of this pathetic Swede really necessary? I've little time for the Swedish. They flip-flop between us and the enemy like miserable cowards.'

'Quite, Herr Obergruppenführer, however Doctor Månsson is an expert in his field. I think you will be impressed.'

The stormtroopers moved to either side of the room now, leaving the prisoner alone and exposed. He wore only a pair of loose-fitting trousers and an equally baggy over-shirt which was torn and hung open, exposing his painfully thin torso and protruding ribs. One of Wolfensohn's entourage took a photograph, and the flash startled the prisoner as if it had been a gunshot. In his mind he imagined the picture being placed alongside a family photograph he'd had taken several years ago. He had a flickering, fleeting memory of the man he used to be: proud and strong, hard-working, a good father and a loving husband. That man was gone now. All self-worth lost forever. Broken. Bare feet on concrete. Mouth full of ulcers. Muscles full of pain. Piss and blood stains. Hopelessness.

Professor Eisen jabbed a needle into his upper arm, and the prisoner prayed it would bring the blessed relief he craved. The edges of his vision quickly lost focus, and the world became black momentarily. He felt his legs buckle, but he did not feel the fall. Still strung up, little more than a skeleton wrapped in rags, he juddered, twitched and shook, and then was still. Blood-tinged spittle dribbled from the corner of his mouth.

Wolfensohn was not impressed, and wasted no time in letting his displeasure be known. 'Pathetic,' he shouted angrily. 'You bring me all this way, and for what?' He stood up and drew his pistol, pointing it at Eisen then Månsson in quick succession. Eisen cowered, Månsson did not. 'I already know how to kill, you imbeciles.'

'Wait, Herr Obergruppenführer, please,' Eisen said meekly, but Wolfensohn was incensed. He kicked the prisoner's outstretched leg, then emptied several rounds from his Walther P38 into the dead man's chest.

Wolfensohn turned his weapon on Scherler. 'You promised me progress,' he bellowed. 'You said these men had created something which would ensure victory.'

'And they have, Herr Obergruppenführer, look.'

Scherler pointed at the prisoner. Wolfensohn took a step back with surprise. The dead man's hands were twitching in his shackles. His body was broken and his torso filled with lead but, incredibly, he appeared to still be alive. His movements were initially slow and laboured, but regained strength and purpose with each passing second. Soon he was standing completely upright, face-to-face with the stunned SS officer.

'I suggest you move a little further away, Herr Obergruppenführer,' suggested Professor Eisen.

'What? You expect me to give ground to this miserable—'

His words were abruptly truncated when the prisoner launched himself forward with astonishing violence and fury. So violent was his attack that one of his shoulders was dislocated, wrenched from its socket, and yet he appeared oblivious to any pain. Wolfensohn staggered back with surprise, knocking into chairs and almost losing his balance. The prisoner craned and strained to get free, clawing at the air, desperate to get at him.

'This is... impossible,' Wolfensohn said. 'How can this be?'

'With respect, Herr Obergruppenführer,' Eisen said, 'the science is rather too complex to explain. Suffice to say, Månsson and I have between us developed a method to defer death... to imbue the dead with the control of the living.'

'It's a relatively simple process, actually,' Månsson began to explain. 'One just has to identify the chemical compounds responsible for—'

Scherler silenced him with a wave of his hand.

Wolfensohn approached the captive man again, edging nearer, but ensuring he remained just out of reach. 'The implications are vast... incalculable. The Führer will be pleased. This discovery of ours will alter the course of the war.' He edged closer still, as if taunting the reanimated corpse, teasing it. The dead man duly reacted, pulling hard against his shackles. A prisoner showing such fearless dissent when facing a senior SS officer – it was unheard of.

'An undefeatable army,' Wolfensohn mused. 'A soldier who cannot be killed because he is already dead, a warrior who acts without fear or hesitation... the enemy will have no answer to an unstoppable force such as this.'

'It is more than that, Herr Obergruppenführer,' Eisen said. 'Witness the full change in our subject's character. Just a few minutes ago, this man barely had the strength to hold up his own head. Now look at his fury. Look at his anger. His *hatred*.'

Wolfensohn glanced back at the rest of the room. Some of his underlings were nodding and agreeing obediently. Others seemed quite unable to process everything they were witnessing.

In the brief moment Wolfensohn was distracted, the dead man lunged again. This part of Polonezköy was dilapidated and rarely used, and the unnatural strength of the corpse was sufficient to yank several rusted screws from the plaster and brick wall. A few extra inches of reach was enough, and the emaciated cadaver grabbed hold of Wolfensohn. The two of them stumbled down to the ground together. The SS officer was caught off-guard, but fortunately the prisoner was yanked back by the one arm still chained to the wall. The dead man's teeth snapped inches from Wolfensohn's face, spraying blood-tinged spittle. The Nazi forced one leather-gloved hand up and gripped tight the crazed creature's painfully thin neck. He hefted the body up and away, helped by SS-Unterscharführer Ruprecht Weigle who happened to be standing in the wrong place at the wrong time. All Weigle wanted to do was run, but the consequences of failing to help the Obergruppenführer did not bear thinking about.

Scherler tried to help Wolfensohn up, but the senior officer brushed him away and used an upturned chair for support instead. He stood upright and cursed the state of his once-impeccable uniform, now drenched with the dead prisoner's rancid blood.

'The tenacity of this monster is remarkable,' Wolfensohn said. Even now the damn creature was still struggling, still fighting to escape its bonds.

Professor Eisen crept forward again. 'Do you understand now, Herr Obergruppenführer? We can create a race of super-soldiers which are impervious to pain and which want nothing more than to kill.'

Wolfensohn, his composure returning, pointed at SS-Unterscharführer Weigle. 'I want to see you fight that creature. One on one.'

'But sir...'

Wolfensohn was in no mood for dissent. He glared at one of the stormtroopers who'd chained the prisoner to the wall. 'Remove his chains,' he ordered, 'and the rest of you keep back. I want to gauge the ability of Professor Eisen's creation.'

Without hesitation, a bubble of space formed around SS-Unterscharführer Weigle. The shackles were removed, and the prisoner came straight at him. Weigle side-stepped, and the dead man flew into the space where the young Nazi had just been, then kept going and collided with the wall. His head left a bloody mark on the grubby plaster, but his injury seemed not to bother him in the slightest as he turned around on leaden feet and fixed Weigle in his sights again.

Weigle had a new-found confidence now. Buoyed up by his opponent's slothful reactions, he wondered whether this was as dangerous a situation as he'd originally thought. The dead prisoner came at him a second time and, once again, he was able to slip out of the way.

'I ordered you to fight the prisoner, not dance with him.'

Nervous laughter echoed around the room in response to Wolfensohn's jibe, but Weigle wasn't laughing. He had his rifle ready now, and as the dead man came at him for a third time, he opened fire.

It was the prisoner's speed which caught him off-guard. Although he blasted the man's pelvis and one knee, and hit him in the neck and once more in the chest, the drug-fuelled monstrosity had enough forward momentum to keep coming through the gunfire. The prisoner grabbed hold of Weigle, gripped his tunic tight, then pulled himself close enough to sink his yellowed teeth into the unterscharführer's neck. Blood poured from the vicious wound and the Nazi dropped to the ground, buried under the dead man's relentless attacks.

With a casual nonchalance, Wolfenson grabbed the prisoner by the scruff of his neck and lifted him up. He continued to twist and writhe, but the Nazi's strength was sufficient to keep snapping jaws at bay. He raised his Walther again, held it to the dead man's temple, and blew a hole in his head. He immediately became limp – as if a switch had been flicked – and the Obergruppenführer dropped him and wiped his bloody hands. 'Most interesting...' he said as he paced the room. Scherler and Professor

Eisen followed close behind, scurrying after him nervously. He stopped. 'There is some potential here.'

'Forgive me, Herr Obergruppenführer,' the professor said, sounding nervous yet excited, 'but there is more than just potential. Our work *will* change the direction of the war.'

The Nazi turned to face the professor who visibly cowered. Despite being several inches shorter than the willowy scientist, his aggression, rank and physical strength was clearly intimidating.

'Professor Eisen, may I remind you that almost the entire world is presently at war. May I also remind you that there are many directions on a compass.'

'I do not follow...'

'A change of direction is one thing, but do not allow your parlour games, as impressive as they may be, to give you a false sense of security. The direction we take must be the direction the Führer wishes us to take. We must not be hasty and choose the wrong option.'

'But Herr Obergruppenführer—'

'This serum you have developed,' Wolfensohn continued, 'it has potential, but I also foresee risks. We must maintain control.'

'Herr Obergruppenführer, I can assure you that we will have full control of—'

Wolfensohn roughly shoved Eisen to one side and fired his pistol directly into the pallid face of dead Unterscharführer Weigle who was now back up, coming at them on unsteady feet, a hair's breadth from attacking the professor. Wolfensohn's aim was dead-on and the back of Weigle's head exploded crimson against the grey plaster wall.

'Professor Eisen, I do not believe you can assure me of anything just yet. I have seen enough to appreciate the potential of this development, but potential alone will not win us the war. You will leave with us for Berlin tonight and continue your work there.'

'Of course, Herr Obergruppenführer, but I have all I need here. Månsson and I have adequate facilities and all the bodies we need for experimentation. Please allow me to remain here...'

Eisen stopped talking, because it was clear that Wolfensohn wasn't listening. He'd turned his back and was already on his way out of Polonezköy.

BASTOGNE
LATE DECEMBER 1944

Lieutenant Joseph Coley of the 394th Regiment, 99th Infantry Division, was as sick of Bastogne and Belgium and of this whole damn war as it was possible for a man to be. He'd seen such things over the last days and weeks as he never could have imagined, and he wondered if there was any chance of normality ever being restored to his life again. It certainly didn't feel that way. Right now it felt like he was on another planet, like he'd need a rocket-ship to get back home again.

Bastogne was in ruins. It had been an unexpected pressure point in an equally unexpected battle. The Nazis had launched a sweeping offensive across Belgium and taking this place, where the seven main roads through the Ardennes converged, was a key strategic aim, integral to the German plans to push on and take Antwerp. The fighting here since mid-December had been hellish, the besieged population brought to their knees with many of their homes and buildings reduced to rubble.

War is never an exact science, but what happened in Bastogne was beyond the plans and expectations of even the most experienced and war-wise military tacticians. To have had to defend the town against an unexpected enemy surge from one source was testing enough for the allies, but when faced with a second, almost unearthly enemy, the odds of victory had been slashed to all but zero.

Coley had seen countless nightmarish things when he'd last been here, just a few days earlier. Back then, the controlled destruction of a part of the town was just about sufficient to hold back the inhuman army which the allies had faced. Huge, mountainous piles of crumbled masonry had blocked the way and prevented most of them from getting through. But there had been reports that another great wave was on its way, and Coley had headed back with his men to shore up. *Seven roads into Bastogne*, he remembered, *seven ways for them to come at us*.

Fighting krauts was one thing – fighting this new threat was another thing altogether. He and his men were already against the ropes before he'd seen what their new enemy was capable of. They'd fought tooth and nail to defend their position, their supplies and ammo running dangerously low, and just as it had seemed that all was lost, the balance shifted. They'd witness the unimaginable – German against German, an enemy mutating and consuming itself – but no matter how it impossible it seemed, it had happened.

Coley and his men had made it out of the blood-soaked chaos alive and had taken a handful of German POWs to boot. One of them, Erwin von Boeselager, of the 9th Fallschirmjaeger Regiment, 3rd Fallschirmjaeger Division, was still with him now. This new threat was such that the bitterest of enemies were forced to work together in order to avoid defeat.

Von Boeselager told Coley what he'd known about the situation. He explained that an experimental serum had been developed with the intention of making Nazi soldiers stronger and faster, and whilst there had been some limited success on that score, the devastating side-effects negated all of the potential Nazi gains. It was hard to believe that something of such apparent insignificance had had such a remarkable impact. In a world where the calibre and explosive strength of a weapon had been a precursor to dominance, it seemed perverse to think that so much damage had been inflicted by mere chemical compounds. Molecules so minute that they couldn't be seen with the naked eye; so much destruction wrought by something which was as good as invisible to man. Too small to see, and too small to defend against.

The Nazi warmongers hadn't stopped to consider the implications of what they'd unleashed. Wave after wave of crazed, barely controlled, undead soldiers had swarmed through the surrounding region and into Bastogne, and had changed the direction of every hand-to-hand battle in which they were involved. They demonstrated a ruthless combination of traits: no fear, unflagging energy, an inability to feel pain, and absolutely no concept of mercy. Men, women and children, young or old, soldier or civilian, all were targets. And if that wasn't enough, Coley and von Boeselager had witnessed even more terrifying behaviours. The undead army attacked indiscriminately, regardless of nationality or allegiance. Most worryingly of all, the contagion which had turned these people into vicious, driven killers with a taste for fresh human flesh, was transmitted to their prey through every bite and scratch. The victims of the undead *became* the undead. People were attacked, killed and conscripted in one fell swoop.

The ever-growing army kept coming, and the allies needed to keep plugging the gaps.

Higgins, late of the 969th Field Artillery Battalion, accompanied Lieutenant Coley alongside von Boeselager and another German, Mathias Altschul, as they rattled along the road back into Bastogne in a battered jeep that had seen better days. Altschul had fled the undead scourge and surrendered to the Americans. In the circumstances, given that the first US troops he'd encountered whilst on the run still had a pulse and the propensity for rational decision making, waving the white flag had seemed the most sensible choice. When you'd been fighting an enemy so hard for so long, however, sudden changes of priority were hard for all concerned to swallow. Higgins leant forward to whisper to Coley. 'Don't feel right, Lieutenant, sitting here with a pair of krauts.'

'Kraut or no kraut, these boys have both got a heartbeat and an off switch. And Mr von Boeselager here helped me out of a scrape, let's not forget that. I'm under no illusions, son, I know what's at stake. We need to focus more on what we've got to do, less on who we're doing it with.'

It didn't sit well, but Higgins knew he was right.

Bastogne was like the Hoover Dam, and they were there to plug the leaks. That was how Lieutenant Coley explained it. Whilst the town had been liberated, the undead army just kept coming. The ruined buildings and blocked streets were just about keeping them at bay, but sometimes the pressure got too much and they broke through. 'We're a repair crew,' Coley told them, 'here to help stop those leaks becoming a flood.'

The lieutenant's analogy was apt. At the point they'd been ordered to defend this morning, two buildings had been destroyed, one on either side of one of the roads out of town, all but completely blocking the way through. A 155mm howitzer had since been used to strike the area from a distance, but a stray round had punched a hole in the debris, leaving enough of a gap for an unsteady stream of the undead to pile through. Now Coley and his men stood a short way away, picking off the advancing enemy with M1 carbines.

'It's like a goddam shooting gallery,' Higgins shouted to Coley, and he was right. As the undead appeared – forced over the rubble peaks by the sheer mass of animated bodies following behind – Coley took pot-shots. The distance gave him a few seconds to compose himself and take aim, and it was never anything less than completely satisfying to see the back of some undead kraut's head explode outwards from a direct hit. Higgins' action was far more frantic, spraying lead at anything that moved. 'Twenty-three, twenty-four...'

'You are keeping count?' Altschul said, sounding disgusted. 'This is not a game.'

'Sure ain't. I just enjoy counting how many Nazis I get rid of. Something to tell the kids.'

'Focus, Higgins,' Coley ordered from over to his right.

Altschul did his best to ignore the American's banter, and to put from his mind the fact that most of these men – these *creatures* – they were destroying had once been his fellow countrymen. Had he known any of them before they'd been corrupted and mutated like this? Had he trained alongside them? How close had he himself been to becoming like this, and could it still happen?

Distracted, he allowed his rifle to jam. It took only a few seconds to be ready to fire again, but by then one of the dead was almost upon him. The creature had a vile expression on its twisted face: absolute hatred. Its speed increased as it approached him, hands reaching out as if it couldn't wait to grab him and tear him to pieces.

Two things saved Altschul – the fact the cadaver lost its footing in the rubble and stumbled, and the single well-aimed shot from von Boeselager which pretty much blew the damn thing's head clean off its shoulders.

'I said focus,' Lieutenant Coley warned.

But Altschul was really struggling. Struggling with the pressure, struggling with the relentless nature of the apparently endless attack, and struggling with the fact that the corpse coming at him now couldn't have been more than ten years old when he'd died. A small boy, wearing pyjamas soaked with blood, most of the skin and hair burned away from the right side of his head. Altschul fired, and his shot missed and ricocheted off a lump of masonry. He wiped his face and aimed again, but all he could think was that the child looked like his brother Rudolph's youngest son. The family lived in Würzburg. He was looking forward to seeing them again, once this damn war was over...

'Altschul!' Coley screamed at him.

Altschul heard him, but he could barely focus now, could hardly think straight. He lowered his weapon and staggered back, tripping over a rubble-buried kerb and ending up on his backside looking up, watching helplessly as the dead boy continued his advance. From the biggest soldier to the smallest child, they all had the same emotionless gaze and inexorable intent. He kicked out when the child was close, and booted him square in the chest, sending him flying. Altschul could only see the face of his nephew Peter now, and immediately regretted his action. He picked himself up and almost went to help the dead child, now oblivious to the raging gunfight which continued all around him. Coley and Higgins were just about managing to hold back the tide of dead flesh, but they were one man down and losing their advantage. More of them were coming through the gap all the time, and the two Germans were no longer firing. Von Boeselager was moving out to the side. 'I will try to block the way through,' he yelled, struggling to make himself heard over the noise. He climbed up onto another mound of rubble which had once been a house, then ripped the pin from a grenade and lobbed it over towards the gap. It detonated with a deafening crack which echoed off the walls of the few buildings which remained standing. Body parts flew in all directions, and a dirty red mist filled the air momentarily. When the dust and debris cleared he saw that he'd succeeded in partially stemming the flow, but more of the dead were still getting through, piling forward with savage intent and no concern for their own physical safety, dragging themselves over what remained of their fallen brethren.

Higgins stopped firing momentarily, distracted by plumes of dust and a shower of broken brickwork which fell from the top floor of a townhouse. The building looked like it had been pounded with artillery fire for days on end and yet, somehow, it remained standing. It was like a movie set: an empty façade, propped up and giving the illusion that normal life continued within its hollow walls. 'Careful,' he warned the German. 'That place don't look too steady to me.'

But von Boeselager wasn't listening. He was still focussed on stopping the flow of the river of death. He hurled another grenade and it detonated on the far side of the rubble-strewn gap, close to the dilapidated building.

There was a moment of deceptive calm. It was over as quickly as it had begun.

'Jeez... everybody outta here!' Lieutenant Coley hollered, because it was clear that what they'd feared happening had just been triggered. The propped up building wall had been damaged at its base, and the little structural integrity the battered old place offered had just been taken away. It began to topple forward, falling like a book on the end of a shelf. 'Run! Now!' the lieutenant screamed.

His men didn't need to be warned again. They sprinted as fast as they could, but between the dead and the countless obstacle-like remnants of war left everywhere, their progress was terrifyingly slow. Tonnes of masonry began to crash to the ground, crushing many corpses but also releasing many, many more. They surged forward again, from numerous different directions now.

Von Boeselager grabbed Altschul's arm and tried to drag him away, but his countryman had been reduced to a mere shell of a man, traumatised by all he'd seen. The undead child had been the final straw, and he was simply unable to cope with the wave after wave of decay which now rolled towards him. He stood his ground and continued to fire fruitlessly into the advancing hordes, but there were too many for him. They soon swarmed over him in massive numbers, digging their teeth and fingers into his unprotected skin, and ripping his flesh from his bones.

His agony was brought to an abrupt end when a massive chunk of balustrade dropped from a height and obliterated him and the best part of twenty crazed corpses.

The rest of the collapsing building was falling in on itself now. Higgins tripped as he tried to run, his foot disappearing down into a crater in the middle of what had once been one of the busiest roads into Bastogne but which was now indistinguishable from the rest of the ruination. His boot was trapped by the debris in the hole, and whilst he tried with all his might to pull himself free, he knew his number was up. He looked up and pointlessly covered his head with his hands as tonnes of brickwork and plaster came crashing down on top of him.

Von Boeselager and Lieutenant Coley kept moving back, helping each other and managing to make it to just beyond the danger zone. 'What have I done?' von Boeselager asked as the deafening, ground-shaking rumble of the building's collapse began to fade, but Coley wasn't in the mood for conversation. The air was filled with slowly sinking clouds of dust. Coley peered through the grit-fuelled smog and saw that much of the building's frontage had fallen at an angle, collapsing like a domino onto a derelict row of houses adjacent, and bringing half of them down too. The net result: a couple of minutes ago they'd had a clear choice of roads out of here and a single weak point to defend, but now their position was wholly different and far more dangerous. Their jeep was gone, crushed, and rubble blocked three ways out, reducing their escape routes to one. And by God, that escape was now a necessity.

'Move,' Coley said to von Boeselager, nerves masking the fear.

'I thought I could stop them. I thought I could prevent them from getting closer and...'

'MOVE!' Coley yelled, and he shoved the German hard between his shoulder blades.

Behind them, behind the mountainous piles of debris, a huge mass of undead bodies had been trapped by chance. They'd been funnelled into an enclosed space through the narrow gap between a church and an abandoned Sherman tank. It had acted like a valve – letting them in, but not letting them back out. The grenade blast and the building collapse had inadvertently released this huge, frenzied gathering of dead flesh.

Von Boeselager glanced back over his shoulder as he ran, and saw the dead spilling through the chaos of the scene and coming after them. Some moved with vicious, almost predatory speed. Some of them, white-suited Nazis, carried weapons, wielding rifles as clubs, seemingly incapable of using them as they were designed. Some of the creatures had, until not long ago, been civilians: innocent victims of the war, now doomed to hunt and kill forever.

Lieutenant Coley ran down the only clear stretch of street, von Boeselager close behind. At the end of a row of battered buildings he took a sharp right and headed along another ruined road. He was vaguely aware of von Boeselager calling after him, but paid him no heed. 'No, Lieutenant, not that way... you're going deeper into the town.'

Coley was running on pure adrenalin now, and he wasn't stopping for anyone, not until he was clear of the hellish hordes still following in dogged pursuit.

Wait.

More of them up ahead.

There were corpses in front of him now, and over to his left too.

He realised too late that he'd run right into the centre of Bastogne's town square. Von Boeselager caught up with him quickly. 'This was a mistake, Lieutenant. You have us backed into a corner.'

Coley gasped for breath. 'Wait, you start throwing grenades around and bring down half the town and set a thousand of those monsters free, and you're lecturing me about making a bad decision?'

'Let us argue about it later, Lieutenant, please.'

The German tried to go back in the direction from which they'd just come, but he quickly stopped. There were more corpses emerging from the mist, their numbers impossible to gauge in the encroaching gloom. And more on the other side of them, too. And across the square. They were coming from all directions, converging on this place.

'Shit,' Coley said. 'Honours even. I reckon we both screwed up.'

Their view from roughly the middle of the town square was disappointingly limited. The buildings were as faceless as the dead: empty façades, gaping black windows and doors which mimicked the emotionless eyes of the undead enemy. Around them there were blackened tree stumps, too badly damaged to climb, and burnt-out vehicles which had been mangled beyond recognition, deformed by explosions and heat.

Coley started to run again, but stopped when he was confronted by an approaching wall of undead figures. Von Boeselager had tried to go the other way, but he too had been beaten back. They met again on one side of the square and stood back-to-back. 'Got any more smart ideas?' Coley asked.

'I have two more grenades,' von Boeselager replied, semi-serious.

'That ain't gonna help much.'

The German turned around and shook Coley's hand. His voice cracked with emotion. 'Thank you, Lieutenant. It has been an honour.'

'Likewise,' Coley immediately replied. 'Now we've both still got our weapons. I reckon we should try and get rid of a few more of these damn things while we still can. The more of them we kill, the fewer we leave for everyone else.'

'Agreed, but promise me one thing.'

'What's that?'

'Save two bullets – one for each of us. I've been fighting the whole war, so I am used to the idea of dying. The idea of not dying and ending up like these poor souls, however, is intolerable.'

'Agreed,' Coley said, and he aimed his M1 into the crowd and fired off a burst of lead. Von Boeselager followed it up with his penultimate grenade.

Coley moved towards the advancing cadavers as he fired, waving his weapon from one side to the other and mowing down scores of corpses. For each one of them that fell, it seemed that countless more were immediately ready to take their place.

He heard something in a brief pause between shots. He looked over at von Boeselager who'd clearly heard it too. There it was again. A wolf whistle. The high-pitched sound cut through the chaos of everything else. Von Boeselager spotted the source and pointed up. Coley peered through the mist, struggling to concentrate as he divided his attention between looking for a way out and keeping more of the dead at bay. 'Over here,' a voice shouted. It sounded miles away, but it wasn't. Coley eventually saw a figure at a top-floor window, waving furiously. A corpse lurched angrily at the lieutenant, wrong-footing the soldier and getting far too close for comfort, but it was dispatched quickly with a single sniper shot. The back of its head exploded outwards like a balloon filled with crimson-red paint.

Now it was von Boeselager's turn to take the lead. 'Come on,' he said, and he dropped his shoulder and ran headlong into the mob of bodies which had filled the space between their current position and salvation. Coley followed closely, but his legs were tired and each forward step was an effort. He could feel every pace through the worn out soles of his boots, and though it seemed a way out was close at hand, the nearer they got, the farther they seemed to be.

'Over the wall,' a voice shouted to them, and Coley was relieved to hear a Brooklyn accent. The thought had struck him that he might be about to put himself at the mercy of a lone pocket of Nazis, but even living Nazis were better than the foul dead things which swarmed around them. Everywhere he looked he saw their horrific, bloodied faces glaring back at him. It was only their comparative individual slowness which allowed him and von Boeselager to get through. Their reactions were dulled somewhat. *Maybe the longer they're dead, the harder it is for them to keep functioning?* he thought to himself.

There was someone down at ground level to help, thank God. Coley could see him straddling the low wall they were running towards, his legs tucked away on the safe side. He reached out for von Boeselager and helped him up and over, and Coley was about to stretch his arms up when he felt dead fingers clawing at his back. Several of the creatures grabbed his tunic and he was pulled backwards, deeper into the decaying crowd. A spray of gunfire came from up high, thinning the crowd out sufficiently so that two more soldiers could vault over the wall and help the lieutenant to safety. One of them carried a bowie knife and he moved from corpse to corpse to corpse, grabbing each of them in turn by the scruff of the neck, plunging the blade into their temple, then dropping them down again. 'Don't know how the hell you do that so fast, Escobedo,' his colleague remarked.

When sufficient numbers of corpses had been beaten away, the men helped Coley over the wall and into the ruin of a building in which they'd been hiding. Coley climbed the rickety stairs without question or hesitation, figuring that whatever was waiting for him up top couldn't be any worse than what he'd just escaped down at ground level. He caught up with von Boeselager at the top of the steps. The German had his arms raised in surrender. 'It's okay,' Coley said, breathless. 'He's with me. He's on our side.'

'A damn kraut?' an older-looking soldier asked from across a spacious, but largely empty room. The man lovingly cradled a Remington M1903, no doubt the weapon which had saved Coley's bacon a couple of minutes earlier.

'Yes, soldier,' Lieutenant Coley said. 'A damn kraut.'

'Now let's not get off on the wrong foot here, fellas,' another man said from the opposite corner of the room. He stepped forward and saluted, then made a point of shaking both Coley's and von Boeselager's hands. 'I'm Jim Parker, late of the 101st.'

'Good to see you, Lieutenant,' Coley said. 'Joe Coley, 99th Infantry Division.'

'Good to see you too.' Parker gestured at the sniper by the window. 'This here's Kenny Gunderson, and these young fellas who escorted you upstairs to our luxury abode are Escobedo and Johnson.'

'The help was appreciated, gentlemen,' Coley said. 'We got ourselves into something of a spot out there.'

'That you did,' Parker agreed. 'But it's no great surprise. Take a look from our birds nest up here.'

The room in which they'd gathered was on the third floor of a block which had been so badly battered by artillery fire that it felt like it was swaying in the cold winter wind. Coley realised that was an illusion, perpetuated by the fact that all the windows in this place had been blown out, allowing every gust and breeze to blow straight through. Although desperately cold and inhospitable up here, its height, combined with the fact that many other buildings in the centre of Bastogne had been flattened in the fighting, gave the men a panoramic view of the devastation in all directions. But it wasn't the ruination Coley was interested in, rather it was the scores of vicious bodies which filled the square below and spilled out into the streets in almost every direction.

Von Boeselager was visibly shaken by what he could see. 'It was enough of a battle to get up here,' he said. 'I cannot imagine how we will ever get out again.'

'Yep,' Escobedo said, sitting in a corner and drawing his legs to his chest to block out the cold as he cleaned his knife, 'that's about the short and the tall of it.'

'Why d'you think we're perched up here like this?' Johnson added. 'If we coulda gone, we woulda gone.'

Coley looked down into the town square from which he and von Boeselager had just made their desperate escape. The amount of dead flesh down there appeared endless, and with the rest of Bastogne all but abandoned, there was nothing else left to distract the infernal army. They weren't going anywhere fast. 'It's like hell on Earth,' he said under his breath.

'That it is, that it is,' Parker agreed. 'I'd like to say you get used to looking at it after a while, but that'd be a lie. You don't. I figure things like this we'll carry to the grave. We've been stuck up here a couple days now and, tell you the truth, I've pretty much stopped my men from looking out. See, the deeper you look, the worse it gets.' He put a hand on Coley's shoulder and pointed down. 'See what I'm saying? Those two down there, they're nothing more than children.'

Coley quickly spotted the two dishevelled creatures he'd been pointing out. Small and blood-stained, they'd clearly failed to escape the fighting which had consumed their town.

'Man, the little ones creep me out,' Escobedo said from down on the floor. 'Ain't no difference between them and the krauts out there.'

'He's not wrong,' agreed Gunderson. 'Don't matter how big or small they are, kid or no kid, find yourself facing one of those damn things and you need to move fast. They'll rip your heart out soon as look at you.'

'There's thousands of them,' Coley said. The scale of the undead army had been apparent from down at ground level, but being up here added a whole new sense of perspective. A sense of perspective he decided he could have well done without.

'And our boys too,' Parker continued, pointing into another part of the crowd where a pack of figures milled in tattered and dust-covered, yet instantly recognisable uniforms. 'Our boys fighting alongside kids and Nazis. I never thought I'd see the day.'

'You must put your preconceptions and prejudices to one side,' von Boeselager said. 'These creatures are on no one's side but their own. Men, women, Americans, Germans, British, young, old... once the effects of the serum have been passed onto them, there is no hope. We are all standing at the very gates of hell. All of us.'

THE FOREST
OUTSIDE BASTOGNE

When Lieutenant Robert Wilkins came around, he was hanging upside-down from a tree. He remembered the drop from the plane – him and many other scouts bundled out of the back of a Dakota in the midst of a massive supply drop, using the falling ammo and other supplies as cover. He remembered his parachute opening, and the rush of air as the rapid descent was arrested. He remembered the wind and the snow and the uneasy panic of being blown wildly off-course and left hanging prone in the air with all hell unfolding on the ground far below him... and then the memories stopped. He was now hanging by his knees over a branch, head down and legs up, blood rushing in the wrong direction. He recalled a viciously swirling gust. A sudden blizzard. Ice pricking his skin like someone was hammering in nails...

Got to move.

It was still snowing, and the uncomfortable angle at which he'd come to rest in the tree made it difficult to move. He considered dropping down, but it was hard to accurately estimate how far it was to fall. The white blanket covering the ground appeared deceptively soft and inviting, but Wilkins knew he couldn't afford to take any risks. Chances were it wouldn't have been anywhere near thick enough to cushion his fall, and there could have been anything beneath the pristine virgin snow: tree roots, a chasm, rocks... anything. He couldn't risk it. He knew the importance of his mission. He knew how much was riding on the success of him and others.

Getting down safely was going to take some skill, and right now Wilkins felt anything but skilful. *This time yesterday,* he thought, *I was back in Blighty with Jocelyn.* He knew he'd so far been fortunate in comparison to so many other people, particularly those here in mainland Europe, but that didn't make the pain of being away from his love any easier to stand.

Wilkins carefully anchored his legs around the thick bough to make sure he didn't fall, then began to swing gently from his hips, weighed down by his pack but hoping to build up enough forward momentum to grab another branch and use it to haul himself upright. The bark dug into the backs of his knees, the discomfort increasing with each upward movement and backwards swing. Arms outstretched, his fingertips brushed against another branch, and then he swung harder again, not knowing how much longer he could keep this up for.

Contact.

He caught hold of the branch with his left hand and held on for all he was worth, stretching his body as far as he could – almost too far – to grab hold with his right. He moved hand over hand to manoeuvre himself closer to the trunk of the tree, then used the trunk to guide himself upright and secure his position.

The biting cold was unbearable, and he felt uncomfortably precarious up here like this. Wilkins wrapped his arms around the tree trunk and hugged it like a long lost friend. Shaking with cold, he clung on for dear life.

Alone in the backwoods of war-torn Belgium in the middle of winter. The dead of night. The sounds of fighting nearby. He was hard pushed to think of a more wretched place to be, and yet it was better to be up here than down there. If his parachute wasn't enough of a giveaway, the trail of footprints he'd inevitably leave in the snow as he ran for cover would lead the enemy straight to him.

Whoever the enemy was.

He'd heard things during the mission briefing which had seemed more at home in that *Frankenstein versus the Wolfman* picture he'd caught last year than in the reality of modern warfare. Dead soldiers walking. *Fighting.* It was like something out of the ghost story books his mother had forbade him from reading in his formative years. For now, however, he tried to put all thoughts of ghouls and monsters from his head and focus on staying out of sight and alive.

Wilkins slowly stood up again and rebalanced himself on the bough. There was a more sturdy-looking branch just above and to his left, and despite his aching bones, with considerable effort he managed to haul himself up and wedge himself into a relatively safe place. He took the slack from the parachute cords and tied himself into position.

Sleep was fleeting and light. The noises of the forest kept him awake – birds and animals, the wind and snow, a stream trickling somewhere in the nearby vicinity (which left him with an almost unbearable urge to relive himself from his branch). And in those few moments when the natural noise subsided, other sounds took their place. The rumble and thump of distant explosions. More planes. Gunfire. Cries for help...

It never stopped. The fighting never bloody well stopped.

Shortly before six, still a couple of hours before sunrise, Wilkins heard something different. It sounded like footsteps, though they were slow and laboured, like those of a wounded animal. Perhaps it was one of his colleagues, he wondered, who'd been less fortunate in their landing than he? Wilkins remained perfectly still on his windswept perch, moving only his eyes to try and see through the miserable shadows of the pre-dawn gloom.

The brightness of the snow seemed to partially illuminate the scene from below. The figure which lumbered into view was a Nazi, that much was clear. The man, perhaps six feet tall and with a stocky, muscle-bound frame, walked with a presumptive arrogance, almost as if he was daring anyone to confront him. Dressed in a white uniform covered with dark patches and stains, he had an extremely pronounced, sloping limp. His good right foot crunched through the inches-deep layer of snow, whilst he was dragging his mangled left foot behind.

Wilkins noticed that the stumbling Nazi left behind a trail of glistening dark liquid which could only have been blood. He'd clearly been injured in battle. Physically wrecked, bleeding profusely... just how was he managing to continue to function in this bitter winter cold? Wilkins was finding it enough of a struggle just trying to sit still and stay warm up here. The enemy soldier (who was now just a couple of feet away from the base of the tree in which Wilkins was hiding) appeared impervious to it all. Wilkins wondered if he was in shock, and whether it was sheer adrenalin which kept him moving forward?

The branch he was sitting on creaked under his weight as he shifted to get a better view. The noise had an effect on the figure below. The Nazi stopped walking and changed direction, swivelling back around and looking for the source of the noise. When the man looked up, Wilkins saw that his face had been badly mutilated in battle. His lower jaw was dislocated, hanging uselessly, and one of his eyes was hard to make out amidst a mass of blood and scarring. Wilkins held his breath and remained completely motionless, and was relieved when, after a few more seconds had passed, the injured Nazi trudged on through the snow.

He must have fallen asleep again, because the noise of an animal burrowing in a bush near the base of the tree woke him up. At least Wilkins thought it was an animal. It was difficult to be sure.

Whatever it was, it was hurt. It dragged itself through the snow-covered undergrowth with an awkwardness and lack of speed which indicated it was no longer in full control of all its faculties. He shifted around as best he could, thinking he should drop down and kill the beast and put it out of its misery. Also, if it loitered too long around the base of his tree there was a real risk it might draw unwanted attention to this place. Wilkins took out his clasp knife and cut the parachute cords, then carefully climbed down.

When the animal crawled out into a patch of daylight between the shadows of Wilkins' tree and its nearest neighbour, he had to bite his fist to stop himself screaming out in horror. The creature on the ground was another Nazi, or what remained of one, anyway. The poor bastard appeared to have been brutally cut in two. How it had happened was of little interest to the British soldier – he'd seen far worse injuries before today and would no doubt see more – instead, he tried to understand how this poor bastard was still alive and continuing to move. Incredibly, when what was left of the Nazi lifted its head and saw Wilkins standing a short distance away, it actually sped up. Wilkins backed away, feeling his guts churn at this most horrific and inexplicable sight. Behind what was left of the mutilated soldier's torso his severed spinal cord thrashed in the snow like a stunted tail. It looked vaguely comical, but the Nazi's clear and vicious intent was no laughing matter.

Wilkins reversed, keeping his distance as the dead man reached out his arms and dragged himself along the ground, moving ever closer. His jaw was a constantly snapping maw. Wilkins saw that the flesh around the man's mouth had been torn away, as if someone had taken hold of his top lip and peeled upwards, removing a painful-looking swathe of skin. He backed up against a tree. No where else to go. The Nazi kept coming towards him.

Realisation dawned. 'What the hell am I doing?'

Wilkins cursed himself for allowing himself to become distracted by the abstract horror of what he was witnessing. He'd heard the stories before he'd parachuted in. He'd known what to expect. He reached down into the snow and picked up a football-sized rock, then dropped it hard on the back of the Nazi's unprotected head. And again. And again. And twice more until the foul creature stopped moving and was finally dead. Wilkins had cracked its skull like an egg, and had done more than enough damage to thoroughly mash and mangle everything contained within.

For a moment the lone British soldier contemplated climbing back up into his tree again and never coming down, but he knew that wasn't an option. He and his colleagues had work to do here.

DEEP IN THE FOREST OUTSIDE BASTOGNE

The scars of war were everywhere he looked. Craters, bodies, burned-out vehicles... Wilkins came upon the remains of a jeep which had ploughed into a tree at such speed that its chassis had virtually wrapped around the trunk. Its driver and passenger remained trapped in their seats, pinned into position by the twisted metal wreck. Wilkins hoped for their sake they'd died on impact and not as a result of the fire which had overwhelmed the accident site. Little of the dead men's bodies remained distinguishable; all traces of their history, rank, allegiance and military record having been burned away. And yet their skeletal, charred faces remained horribly readable. Both of their mouths were frozen midway through never-ending screams of pain. Their burned out eyes looked up to the heavens for an explanation which would surely never come.

It was uncomfortably quiet here. Unexpectedly so. No fighting. Nothing. A dead zone. Wilkins almost began to wish for an enemy encounter to prove he was still alive. Whether it was as a result of the bitter cold, the after-effects of being left hanging from a tree, the hideous creatures he'd seen since landing in the forest, or a combination of all three, he was beginning to doubt his sanity. *Am I the one who has died?* he asked himself. It made marginally more sense to believe that the grotesque, borderline surreal things he'd seen were as a result of serious trauma to his brain. He'd witnessed more than his fair share of unspeakable horrors in numerous places since the beginning of the war, but this was different. This didn't feel right.

He'd been keeping a watch for signs of any of the other Brits, and his heart leapt when he spied parachute material entangled among the lower branches of an oak tree tall enough to be hundreds of years old. He ran towards it at speed, only to find one of his countrymen hanging from a bough and quite dead. It was Graeme O'Neill, a good sort he'd known for some years. Poor bugger. O'Neill had a protruding chin and a distinctive mop of tightly curled and well-oiled hair, so there was no question it was him. From the waist up, he appeared relatively unhurt, but the lower half of his body had been unspeakably defiled.

O'Neill's legs had been stripped of all flesh. Little more than blood-stained bones remained, as if the muscles, nerves and sinews had all been eaten away. Directly beneath the dead Brit, the snow had disappeared from a wide circle of ground approaching two yards in diameter, perhaps even larger. Blood and other unspeakable discharge had soaked the forest floor, and there were countless slushy footprints moving to and from O'Neill's body in numerous directions. O'Neill himself bobbed up and down gently as the branches of the mighty oak rustled in the spiteful winter wind.

All's fair in love and war, Wilkins remarked to himself, but there was nothing remotely fair or decent about what had happened here. O'Neill had, apparently, been tortured without mercy. A degree of hatred and inhumanity towards one's enemy was perhaps to be expected in conflict, but this was something else entirely. This desecration of a fellow soldier's body was senseless. Barbaric in the extreme.

It occurred to Wilkins that whoever was responsible for this most heinous act might still be loitering nearby. However, he owed it to his fallen comrade and his family not to leave him hanging there unceremoniously. He was swinging like an executed man who'd been left on the gallows, chin on his chest and his head hanging heavy on his shoulders. Wilkins looked around and checked that all was clear, then tried to steady the corpse. 'I'm sorry, old boy,' Wilkins said. 'I wish that I could—'

Wilkins jumped back with surprise when O'Neill looked up and fixed him with a gaze from cold and lifeless eyes. Somehow O'Neill's flailing arms caught hold of him and the dead man attempted to take a bite out of Wilkins' hand. Wilkins snatched his hand away and staggered back. By now O'Neill was twitching and bouncing tirelessly on the parachute cords which bound him, spinning around furiously to reach for Wilkins again, but succeeding only in tying himself up in knots. The flesh-free bones of his useless legs clattered together like some bizarre kind of voodoo totem or wind-chime designed to keep evil spirits at bay.

Wilkins didn't believe in evil spirits. Part of him wished he did. Somehow the idea that what was happening here in Belgium could be attributed to the whim of some displeased demi-god was preferable to what he already knew to be the truth. The foul aberrations he'd so far encountered were the result of despicable Nazi experiments. He wanted to run and put maximum distance between himself and this place, but that wasn't an option. Thousands of lives depended on him and the other men who'd baled out over the region during the early hours of this morning. By all accounts, it was no exaggeration to believe that, perhaps, the lives of every last man, woman and child in Europe, if not the entire world were at risk here.

Before he did anything, though, Wilkins knew he had to deal with what was left of O'Neill first. He couldn't leave a fellow soldier hanging up there in such a pitiful state. He took his standard issue clasp knife and, with one hand around O'Neill's throat to keep him steady and keep his snapping jaws at bay, he plunged the blade deep into the dead man's heart.

It had no effect. Absolutely no effect.

If stabbing the heart doesn't do the trick, he thought, *then I have only one other option.*

Wilkins twisted O'Neill's squirming head to the left and stabbed his exposed temple. Almost immediately the dead soldier stopped thrashing and hung from the tree like an abandoned marionette.

Wilkins wiped his knife clean then dug in against the wind and the cold and the pain and the fear in his gut and pushed on towards Bastogne.

AT THE FRONT
NEAR NAMUR

A hole had been punched in the German attack around Bastogne, but the gains made by the allies were bittersweet. The recapture of the town and the end of the siege there had been cause for much celebration, however the hard-fought victory had emphasised the scale of what was left to achieve. The audacious Nazi advance continued west across Belgium and France.

In two days and nights, more than a hundred thousand troops travelled over a hundred miles east under the command of General Patton. They'd known the ensuing battle was going to be hell, but despite all the rumours and reports they'd heard, no one was fully prepared for what awaited them.

The British 6th Airborne and 53rd Infantry Division began to move against the western tip of the German advance, taking up position on the defensive line between Dinant and Namur. As the men fought to force back the Nazis, the terrifying depravity of what was happening elsewhere became clear through radioed reports.

Upon arriving in the area around Christmas the men had, for the briefest time, felt surprisingly festive. It was bitterly cold, and more than six inches of snow had fallen, giving the battlefield a disarmingly calm and peaceful appearance, almost like a greetings card. Securing the town of Bure was the company's first objective, and in no time the illusion of calm had been shattered.

Sergeant Daniel Phillips sprinted down the snow-covered track in pursuit of a group of Nazis who'd so far evaded capture. He was going to get those bastards if it was the last thing he did. He'd left Jack Hewson – his lucky charm who'd been with him every step of the way in this damn war so far – bleeding out having taken a bullet to the chest from one of them. He owed it to Hewson to hunt the bastards down. Never mind that, he *wanted* to do it.

He stopped and took cover against a towering spruce, steeling himself as the tree took several rounds intended for him, feeling the shock travel through the hundred-year-old wood. He crouched down and looked out through the splinters and smoke, then drew his head back in fast when another hail of bullets came his way. Jerry was looking for cover around the back of a grubby cottage on the outskirts of Bure. There were three of them hiding there, maybe even four, but numbers were academic. Phillips was poised to make his move – one last hurrah in memory of Jack – but a well-aimed round from one of the Fife and Forfar Yeomanry's Sherman tanks put paid to any German resistance. The mortar hit the corner of the cottage and brought the whole thing crashing down on top of them.

The area (what was left of it) was secure, and Phillips made his way back deeper into the town. Corporal Charlie Lowell hollered to get his attention and ushered him into a dilapidated house where several other men had gathered to catch their breath. This had been someone's home once, Phillips thought as he looked around the miserable place. It was a cold and empty ruin now, filled with dust and debris and broken glass, little trace of the former occupants visible. 'All right, chaps?' he asked through chattering teeth. It was clear the other men were far from all right. Given their dire circumstances, there could have been any reason for their low mood and dejected nature, but Phillips sensed this was something of the upmost seriousness. Warrant Officer Brian Stewart passed the sergeant a lukewarm drink. Phillips took it but didn't drink. Instead he looked around from man to man, waiting to hear what horrific twist the war had now taken.

Stewart had a wide cockney accent which made him sound chirpy even when he clearly wasn't. 'You ain't heard, Sarge?'

Phillips' blank expression was as good an answer as Stewart needed. 'Heard what?'

Stewart called to another man sitting spread-eagled on the floor in the corner. 'Tell him, Wilson.'

Private Harry Wilson cleared his throat and wiped his face. Phillips had fought alongside him these last few days, and had grown to know him as an effervescent, larger-than-life Yorkshireman. All the verve and vigour had been knocked out of him today, though. 'I overheard it on the radio just a half hour ago, Sarge,' he said, his voice little more than a whisper.

'Overheard what exactly?'

'News from the front, down to the south. The yanks are taking a hammering.'

'The Germans are gaining an advantage? Dammit, I'd heard our boys were fighting them back. General Patton's relieved Bastogne, hasn't he? I know it's been fraught, but the tide's turning, isn't it?'

'It seems the Germans aren't our only problem, these days.'

'What do you mean?' Phillips didn't like the sound of this.

'Have you not heard the rumours about the krauts that don't feel no pain?'

'Rumours, yes... but for goodness sake, the battlefield is a strange place. It can play havoc with a man's sanity. And the human body is capable of all kinds of extraordinary stunts when one's put under extreme pressure. I saw a fellow who'd had his legs clean taken off by a blast managing to run on the stumps. I think it's just a case of...'

The men were staring at him. Phillips stopped talking. Wilson cleared his throat again. 'No, Sarge, that's not what I'm talking about. There's things happening on the battlefield that are evil and unnatural.'

'Go on...'

'I have it on good authority that the Nazis have developed some kind of treatment they're giving their men what's turned them into monsters.'

'Monsters?'

'Aye, sir, monsters. Like I said, I was there listening when the reports was coming in. I know you'll not believe me, but I'll tell you just the same. They're saying these men are already dead, but that this treatment, this serum they've been given, is keeping them mobile and keeping them fighting.'

'That's preposterous.'

'It's true!' Wilson said, and he stood up and moved towards Phillips, decorum and rank temporarily forgotten. 'It's true,' he said again, voice lower, back in control.

Whether or not Wilson and the others had heard the things they were purporting to have heard, it was clear to Phillips that the news had affected each of them deeply. 'Go on,' he pushed.

'These creatures... these dead Germans... they're fighting and fighting and fighting and there's nothing that'll bring them down save for a bullet to the head. Look, sir, I know how mad this must sound, but you should have heard them... you should have heard the panic in our boy's voices.'

'Wilson here reckons that whatever it is that fires these dead blokes up, gets passed on to anyone they kill.' Stewart said. 'Bites, cuts, scratches... Infected blood was what I heard.'

'Wait a minute... let me see if I've got this straight. You're saying Hitler has created himself a self-perpetuating army of monsters?'

'Yes, Sarge, and they're heading our way,' Stewart said ominously.

Phillips stood in the middle of the ice-cold cottage and tried to comprehend what he'd just been told. The building was deathly silent save for the whistling of the winter wind and the rumbling of a tank battle in the near distance.

IN THE RUINS OF BASTOGNE

Most of the population of Bastogne had fled when the siege had ended and the allies had opened a corridor of relative safety between the town and Assenois. *Most* of the population. Some had been unable to get away, others too scared to move until their hand was forced. Henri Mercel, who had, up until a couple of weeks ago, been a well-respected and oft-frequented tailor, ran through the rubble-strewn streets as if his life depended on it.

Because it did.

It had been such a foolish and unnecessary mistake to make, and now he cursed himself for having been so vain. Even after all the horror, brutality and bloodshed he'd witnessed here recently, he'd learnt nothing and had continued to give undue importance to his business and its associated frippery. And now it seemed his misguided approach was going to cost him everything.

When the dead army had begun to surge through the town, Mercel had initially run as fast as anyone, despite his rotund belly and short legs. But it had occurred to him that he'd left a good amount of money and numerous trinkets unguarded in his shop, including a valuable broach bequeathed to him by his recently deceased mother, and the thought of them falling into someone else's hands – British, American, German or other – was intolerable. Against his better judgement he'd cut through an alleyway and doubled-back. He'd simply collect his belongings then disappear again. What was the worst that could happen?

Take the worst that could happen, and multiply it by a factor of several hundred.

Being caught in the cross-fire between the Nazis and the US soldiers defending Bastogne had been bad enough, but what had followed had been immeasurably worse.

The dead.

Hundreds of them, possibly even thousands. Foul, obnoxious, ill-mannered things, their numbers ever growing. Mercel had made it back to his tailor's shop, but only by the slimmest of margins before the ungodly army had filled the street outside. The mass of dead flesh had clogged every escape route. He'd sunk to the ground behind the counter and covered his ears and screwed his eyes shut as the unnatural encroachment had continued. Their numbers had been such that they had blocked out almost all the light, leaving him more frightened than ever. Mother had always been there before to keep him company and help him cope with his irrational fear of the dark, but Mercel was completely alone now. And despite being in his late forties, he was resolutely terrified.

He'd remained curled up on the floor in a ball for hours. It might even have been longer than a day. It was only when an unavoidable call of nature forced him to get up and visit another part of the shop did he see that the street outside had all but emptied. Once his ablutions were complete he filled his pockets with the money and trinkets he'd risked his life for, took a deep breath, then left the shop and ran (as best he could).

It was cold outside, and the snow was falling heavily. The covering of white combined with the absolute ruination in parts of Bastogne to disorientate Mercel to such an extent that he headed in completely the opposite direction to that which he'd originally intended. His choice of direction was further limited by the great crowds of blood-stained and battle-worn Nazis which seemed to be on the periphery whichever way he turned.

At one point he found himself face-to-face with a fellow countryman who appeared to have been completely traumatised by the bloody chaos which had consumed the town. The man had been severely injured (his dust-covered trousers glistened with blood which continued to seep from a vicious-looking wound on his belly) and his shock was such that he couldn't speak, could barely even focus his eyes on Mercel. 'We must leave here, Monsieur,'

Mercel had said. 'Can you help me get to Assenois? I can pay you...'

He'd shown the man a pocket full of francs, and the desperate fellow had made a sudden and unexpected lunge for Mercel's cash. He'd gripped his arms with a dogged persistence which belied his moribund state, and Mercel had struggled to free himself. In the melee he'd slipped on ice then tripped over rubble and had been on his back with the wounded man bearing down on him before he'd known what was happening.

A priest came to his aid.

Father Jacques had elected to remain with his church despite the rest of the town being evacuated, and seeing the overweight tailor struggling in the snow with his assailant was proof positive that staying behind to care for the last few sheep of his flock had been absolutely the right thing to do. His vestments keeping him warm and a pair of hobnail boots keeping him safe, he strode out from the church with a heart full of God and the very best of intentions. When the man attacking Mercel had failed to respond to his requests to desist, Father Jacques put a hand under each of his shoulders and dragged him away.

The good Samaritan paid the ultimate price for his selfless act. The wounded man turned on the priest with predatory speed, reversing their position and slamming Jacques against the outside wall of his church before biting into his throat and crunching through his oesophagus, silencing his screams before they'd even begun.

Mercel was up and on his feet and running again before the priest was dead. He stumbled into a street so heavily bombed that he struggled to place it at all. A street name lying on the ground helped him fix his location, but the familiar view he associated with that name had been all but obliterated. There were gaps where there used to be buildings, like a mouthful of rotten teeth, and those homes and shops which still remained standing seemed to be doing so by the grace of God alone. Mercel fancied that if he was to lean too heavily against any one of them, the whole town might come crashing down around him.

There were mountainous, snow-capped piles of rubble everywhere, and deep puddles where impact craters had become filled with dust and ash and melted snow to leave a claggy, paste-like mud which coated everything. He looked down at his shoes and the bottom of his trousers with real disappointment. He would never normally have allowed himself to be seen out in public in such a bedraggled state.

It was while Mercel was staring at his shoes that he realised the area was splattered with blood and body parts. The remains of people mixed freely with the remains of the buildings they'd previously inhabited, and it was a gruesome sight which caused his stomach to flip. He'd not eaten this morning (not as much as a normal morning, anyway), and it took all the self-control he could muster not to vomit and further ruin his already grubby shoes. But when he caught sight of a hand and part of a forearm, flesh clearly having been chewed and bones snapped just above the wrist, his limited self-control was lost. Mercel emptied the contents of his stomach onto the pavement with a semi-solid splatter, the noise and taste of which did little more than make him heave again. He'd never had the strongest of constitutions, and Mother had always been there to hold the bowl whenever he'd been ill. The fear and isolation caused him to wail for help like a little girl.

In the otherwise all-consuming silence of this dead part of this dead town, his noise travelled a surprising distance. Far enough to be heard by those few people still sheltering in the ruins, and by many *things*.

A scream was a scream, thought Wilkins. Though he'd have rather heard friendly voices and local accents, right now any noise (as long as it wasn't German) was better than no noise at all. He left the cover of the trees and ruined buildings and broke into a gentle jog along the road into Bastogne.

Wilkins sensed he wasn't alone.

He'd seen more and more of them the closer he'd got to town, and here there were hundreds. Driven, faceless, emotionless creatures. Dead soldiers and dead civilians, all fighting for a horrific new army, all as keen as he was to find the lone survivor who'd cried out in fear or pain or both.

***

Lieutenant Parker watched the pitiful man through his binoculars from up high. He lowered the glasses. 'Damn fool's gonna get us all killed at this rate.'

'So whadda we do?' Kenny Gunderson asked. 'Take him out?'

'That ain't exactly playing by the rules, Gunderson, much as it would please me greatly at the present time.'

'So just leave him to it?'

'Ain't you got a single bone of compassion left in your body?'

'Not today, Lieutenant.'

'Look,' Parker said, his interest piqued. 'He's already calling them to him. See how they're drifting? They're moving like a herd of cattle.'

Lieutenant Parker was right. They could all see it. The Belgian's noise was attracting the attention of a huge number of the cadavers still gathered in the square outside. It was like a chain reaction rippling through the masses. Heads were turning on the outer fringes of the huge pack, and those closest to his location were moving away to investigate. 'We're gonna have to go down and get him,' he announced.

'I'll go,' Lieutenant Coley volunteered.

'Appreciate that, but I'd like you up here keeping tabs on your German friend, make sure he don't get up to nothing he shouldn't.'

'I'll go, sir,' Escobedo said, knife ready.

'That's what I like about you, Escobedo. Volunteering before I can volunteer you.'

'Yeah, well I fancied a walk.'

'You too, Johnson.'

'I figured as much,' Johnson said, less enthusiastic.

'I'll provide the downstairs cover, Gunderson'll keep you both safe from up here.'

'Damn right,' Gunderson said, readying his rifle. 'More than happy to do my part and get rid of a few more of them.'

'Just the dead ones and any stray Nazis, Gunderson,' Lieutenant Parker warned.

Henri Mercel was aware of them closing in from all directions. Everywhere he looked he saw them, and there was no question that they had seen him. Trudging and trampling. Moving with lethargy but no lack of intent. Desperate, he crawled under the wreck of an upturned Panzer. Its gun turret had wedged in the mud, leaving just enough space for him to hide and remain out of the reach of grabbing hands. And he knew what damage those grabbing hands could do too. Whenever he closed his eyes to try and block out the immediate horror of his surroundings, all he could see was that poor priest who'd helped him being brutally eviscerated.

The crowd seemed to be thinning out the longer he was out of sight. Had he confused them by disappearing, or had they found another poor soul to hound instead? One of the dead things lost its footing and hit the ground next to him with a nauseating thud, like meat on a butcher's slab. Mercel caught his breath when he recognised the monster.

'Monsieur Lefebvre?'

He immediately cursed his own stupidity in speaking out, but he'd been taken completely by surprise when he'd recognised one of his neighbours. An ex-resident of Bastogne, Monsieur Lefebvre had, until a few days ago, been a quiet and inoffensive boulanger whose shop had been a little way down the street from his own. Monsieur Lefebvre's transformation was remarkable and terrifying. Now he was base and degraded, just like all the rest of them. Blood-soaked and blood-thirsty. The old man dragged himself closer on his belly through the snow, and Mercel saw that his right leg was mangled, broken bones jutting through rips in the flesh. It turned his stomach (again). He screwed his eyes shut, then opened them when he felt Monsieur Lefebvre's cold hands on his feet. He kicked out at the elderly boulanger and, quite by chance, cracked him across the jaw. Another bunny-kick broke the old man's nose. Three more in quick succession and Monsieur Lefebvre was no more. Unfortunately for Mercel, unsighted as he was beneath the Panzer, he hadn't bargained on the effect his uncharacteristic show of resistance would have on the rest of the undead nearby. Almost as one they turned and converged on the wrecked tank, and as the forest of feet and legs grew ever closer, Mercel curled up into a ball again and tried to pretend that none of this was happening.

Escobedo climbed over the wall and landed in the slushy snow on the edge of the town square. Johnson followed close behind. 'What the hell's that no good idiot doing?' he whispered, watching Mercel squabbling with the undead.

'Heads down, fellas,' Lieutenant Parker hissed from over on the other side of the wall, and he ripped the pin and threw a pineapple grenade as far as he could across the square.

A couple of seconds of silence, then the blast. Body parts were hurled in all directions, and the noise echoed off what was left of the town's walls.

Almost as one, the dead forgot about the cowardly Belgian hiding under the tank and surged towards the blast zone. 'Are those things as stupid as they seem?' Johnson asked.

'Yep, pretty much,' Escobedo said. 'Don't matter how dumb they look though, they know how to fight and they know how to bite.'

Parker appeared over the wall again, looking like one of those Mr Chad cartoons the Brits were so fond of (*wot no action?*). 'The hell are you two waiting for? GO!'

Escobedo led the charge. With most of the creatures heading away, it was comparatively easy to get around them. Johnson took out a couple of stragglers with a knife to the nape of the neck (a tip he'd picked up by chance that had unquestionably helped him stay alive). Escobedo followed suit, and the two of them were at the Panzer wreck in no time and with relative ease.

Mercel, however, panicked at the sight of military boots. It was only when Escobedo crouched down and offered his hand that he realised these men were here to help him, not kill him. He gratefully took the soldier's hand and squeezed back out from under the wreck. He stood up and brushed himself down, still breathing, but heartbroken at the state of his jacket and trousers. *'Bonjour...'* he stammered, fishing in his pocket for a white handkerchief to wave in case there was any doubt as to his intention to surrender. *'Je suis tres desole. Je suis—'*

'Nice to meet you, sir. Please shut up.'

'We got company,' Johnson warned. He had his rifle raised ready. The shadows were beginning to swarm back towards them. Hundreds of them.

The close proximity of the dead soldiers elevated Mercel's panic to new heights. He tried to squirm free from Escobedo's grip and get back under the tank. Escobedo again implored him to shut up and calm down, but he was too delirious to listen. He became even more frantic when Kenny Gunderson started picking off more of their would-be attackers from the top floor window.

Mercel flapped and moaned and fought, and only became silent when Escobedo laid him out with a well-aimed right-hand slug. It took all the soldier's strength to heft the deadweight up and carry him back towards their top-floor hideout.

The advancing ungodly army became more riled and aggressive with every single gunshot. Some of them were trying to run. Others fought with each other to be the first to get at the retreating Americans. Johnson struggled to contain his mounting terror. 'These damn things don't know when to quit...' he said, and he watched in disbelief as Gunderson took out another with a perfect shot to the side of the head from above, while another one standing alongside continued oblivious as if nothing had happened. It didn't even flinch when its face was covered with a bloody spray of bone and brain matter from its fallen comrade.

Shot after shot after shot. But for every one of them that Gunderson felled, ten more took their place.

'Keep moving, Johnson,' Escobedo said. 'We gotta keep moving.'

The Belgian was beginning to come around. Escobedo lowered him and put a hand over his mouth, pre-empting another stream of frightened gibberish. Immediately alert again, Mercel began to struggle. Escobedo threatened him with his fist, then pointed up to where his colleagues were watching and waiting. Mercel didn't know where he was going or who he was going there with, but he knew it had to be better than this and he stopped arguing.

The advancing undead army was closing in fast. From Lieutenant Coley's high vantage point he'd noticed a very definite quickening of pace. He'd also noticed other things. He'd noticed how some of the huge crowd, mainly those in uniform – Nazi and allied – moved with more speed and purpose than most of the others. Some of them, he also saw, still carried weapons. Was this a vestigial holdover from before they'd been like this, or something more sinister? Were these damn things still capable of fighting soldier to soldier?

The guys on the ground were struggling. They were in danger of being cut off by the dead, isolated like an island. Coley looked over at von Boeselager and caught his eye. They both knew what had to be done and then pounded down the rickety stairs to ground level.

'I asked you fellas to stay up outa harms way,' Lieutenant Parker said as the men appeared on either side of him.

'Thought you could do with a hand,' Coley said, and he immediately started firing his M1 into the advancing hordes.

The combined firepower coming from in and around the ruined building was just about enough to keep the dead at bay, but all involved knew it was nothing more than a temporary reprieve and that when the shooting stopped, the dead would surge at them again. Escobedo reached the wall first and fairly hoisted Henri Mercel over onto the other side. The overweight Belgian's feet kicked furiously as he tried to get himself over. Coley and Parker hauled Escobedo up. Although von Boeselager offered Johnson a hand, he wouldn't take it. 'Don't need help from no kraut,' he said with the venom in his voice of a man who'd spent too long fighting.

'Quick!' von Boeselager shouted. 'They are close!'

It was clear Johnson wasn't going to let him help, so instead he returned to firing into the crowd. The dead were almost up to the wall themselves now with only Johnson's firepower holding them back.

'Get over here, you dumb bastard,' Lieutenant Parker yelled at him, but Johnson was too busy fighting to listen. From here their numbers appeared endless: thousands where he thought there'd been hundreds. He shot more and more of them, as many as he could, but it was never going to be enough. Parker, Coley and von Boeslager screamed at him to back away, but their voices continued to go unheard.

A white-suited Nazi, pock-marked by bullet holes, came at him at speed, bursting out from the masses. Before anyone could react, the crazed creature had dropped Johnson and squatted on his chest. The dead man attacked with predatory speed, tearing the soldier's throat and chest open.

The last thing Johnson saw was Parker reaching out for him over the wall, and Coley and von Boeselager pulling the lieutenant back the other way. 'Get outta here, Lieutenant,' Johnson wanted to say but couldn't. 'I'm done for.'

He'd heard the cries and the gunfire and fighting all right, but he hadn't bargained on the full extent of the effect the noise was going to have on the swarms of deadly creatures still trapped in the ruins of Bastogne.

Wilkins was in trouble and he knew it. *I'll take a hundred krauts over just a handful of these things,* he thought as he skulked through the shadows. The dead were unnatural and unstoppable. He'd been warned to expect as much, but seeing it with his own eyes was a different matter altogether. He'd witnessed horrifically damaged and disfigured bodies continuing to fight with the venom and animosity of an entire Nazi Einsatzgruppen.

His pistol was useless – more trouble than it was worth. He'd already established that the creatures reacted to noise, and he knew that to fire his weapon out in the open like this would be tantamount to suicide; a kamikaze act (to coin a painfully relevant phrase he'd picked up from recent briefings back home), but one which would result only in his death and not in any perceived tactical gain.

He had to get up off ground level. Being down here was killing him. The vast numbers of the dead limited his visibility to an extraordinary extent and he knew that putting a little distance between him and *them* would help immeasurably. More than that, his speed had now reduced to little more than a painfully slow crawl, matching the slothful movements of the majority of the creatures surrounding him. He'd found that moving this way had, for the time being at least, been enough to convince his unnatural enemy that he was just like the rest of them.

The sounds of nearby fighting (he was sure he could hear Americans shouting) gave him a focus to head towards, but in the chaos of this battle-damaged town, roads had become blocked and routes abruptly truncated by collapsed buildings. He came across one such obstruction unexpectedly, and inadvertently made a sudden about face. He regretted it the moment it had happened, for his deliberate change of direction immediately attracted the attention of a dead woman who tripped along the fringes of another group of bodies. Her cold, emotionless eyes locked on to Wilkins and he felt an icy chill run the length of his spine. She threw herself at him with a sudden burst of speed.

No time to think.

Wilkins took an open door at the front of a house immediately to his left, but immediately found himself outside again, as the building had almost completely collapsed in on itself. But there was opportunity in this wreckage – there had to be! – and he scrambled up the side of an enormous, pyramid-like pile of broken bricks, struggling with the ice and the uneven, constantly shifting surface under his boots. A quick, breathless climb and he was up, walking along what remained of a supporting wall between two terraced homes, balancing with his arms outstretched like an inexperienced tightrope walker at a particularly macabre circus. He ducked through a hole and dropped into a neighbouring building. This one was in a worse state than the first and he could feel its foundations shaking with his every footfall. He knew he was committed. He had to keep moving. Whatever happened next could be no worse than the savage hell he was fleeing.

Wilkins jumped down into what had previously been a family's living room, but was now open to the elements. There was a sideboard where once-prized possessions and framed photographs lay under a covering of dust, snow and ice. It was surreal to see the inside turned outside like this, but Wilkins forced himself to ignore the distractions and keep moving, still listening out for the sounds of the battle nearby.

This dilapidated house had become something of a puzzle; a maze where nothing was where it should have been. In the next room, the upstairs was downstairs. A heavy, wooden-framed bed was sitting uncomfortably astride a few sticks of wood which had, until the shells had hit, been a relatively grand dining suite.

Out of one door and in through the next.

He was closer now, but the gunfire had stopped and the fighting was over. Was he too late?

He threw himself across a narrow alleyway which was swarming with the dead. His speed and strength seemed to take all of them by surprise, and though several tried to grab at him, he was too fast and too strong. He burst through another door into the next building along, only then stopping to think what might have happened had it been locked and he'd been stuck outside with those damned, merciless creatures.

Up again... a staircase which went nowhere. On the top step he took a leap of faith across an unexpected chasm, then ran through the first floor of this building before leaping again, this time from one house to the next. The gap was perfectly manageable, but there was a considerable drop waiting for him, with nothing but the dead to cushion his fall.

There was a church up ahead.

Wilkins used another enormous pile of rubble to climb back down to street level, then ran for all he was worth to reach the grey-stone church. *Sanctuary*, he thought, *in more ways than one*. He weaved through the milling crowds outside, knowing that if he dared slow down or stop, his number would be up.

A Nazi with half its face missing.

A barely-clothed local woman who he might once have found attractive, but whose body was now so consumed with gangrenous rot and decay as to render her completely abhorrent.

A child with a twisted visage who came at him with the ferocity of an SS killer.

A GI that tripped over his own innards which spilled out like glistening paper-chains from an ugly-looking hole in his belly.

A priest who'd had his throat torn out...

The sights surrounding Wilkins were relentless and uniformly horrific. So terrifying, in fact, that he became disorientated again. He reached the church and frantically climbed the steps, but paused before pushing his way inside through the heavy wooden doors. He looked back and surveyed the horrific landscape through which he'd just travelled and wondered if this torture was some kind of divine retribution for the countless lives he'd taken in the name of freedom since this damned war had begun?

The dead were beginning to advance up the steps towards him. He had a couple of second's grace. Many of them struggled with the coordination required to climb.

The church doors were locked. Or blocked. One thing was certain – he wasn't going to get inside.

He listened keenly for some kind of clue which might lead him in the right direction, but there was nothing. As he waited, struggling to keep his composure with so many grotesque ghouls now closing in, he became aware of the horrible noises they made. Dragging feet, but little other sound.

Silence where he'd expected to hear moans and groans. The occasional rattle of air trapped in lungs, and sounds of deflation when one of them hit the ground. Individually he'd have struggled to hear anything, but this was a crowd of incredible proportions, and the cumulative noise was deafening.

Over the chaos, Wilkins heard another brief burst of noise coming from elsewhere. The Americans. One of them screaming. Was he too late?

No time to lose.

He estimated the battle to be taking place somewhere in the region of a quarter of a mile north-east of his current position. He made a note of the various buildings between here and there, then ran like hell; straight back down the steps and deep into the advancing cadavers. He dropped his shoulder and went hell-for-leather, not daring to stop or slow for fear he'd never get moving again and that he'd be overcome by the relentless waves of rot threatening to crash over him from all directions.

A grimy-looking, white-washed building was his next port of call. He entered through a mouth-like hole in a side wall, pursued by an alarming number of staggering corpses. He felt like the Pied Piper in a nightmarish twist on the old folk tale. He lost his footing and fell. His right foot was caught, and he feared for a moment that he might be trapped. He had, in fact, been caught by a grotesquely disfigured soldier who had himself been partially buried under fallen masonry. The soldier had a hold of his boot and was doing all it could to sink its germ-filled teeth into his leg. Wilkins writhed to get away but the creature was deceptively strong and determined, and it took an un-gentlemanly boot to the dead thing's face to free himself. In fact, one boot wasn't enough. Wilkins kicked out again and again, reducing the dead man's face to a virtually unrecognisable pulp. He felt a pang of guilt when he realised the unnatural beast had once been an American soldier. Satisfied he'd done enough to render the poor bastard completely incapacitated, he checked his dog-tags. Private Owen. *What happened to you, Private?* he wondered sadly. *How did you end up here like this?*

Back up and running again, Wilkins weaved around more of the creatures, again slipping through their grabbing hands. He took a sharp right and collided with several more, the force of impact having a greater effect on them than him as they fell like skittles. Another right turn. Still more of them coming from every conceivable angle. So many now that they were all he could see.

And then Wilkins burst out into the open and found himself in the middle of a large space which looked like it had been the scene of the bloodiest of massacres. He was on his own in a decent-sized bubble of space almost at the centre of the area, but his relief was short-lived as the dead came at him from all angles. He could see numerous potential escape routes where there were gaps in and between the battle-damaged buildings, but right now none of them appeared to be viable options. Each exit was choked by throngs of corpses, and it felt like they were all converging on his isolated position. He had about thirty seconds until they swallowed him up, he reckoned, maybe a minute at best.

Sorry, Jocelyn... I tried, but it wasn't enough...

A wolf whistle.

The high-pitched noise was unexpected and strangely directionless as it bounced off the walls of the buildings which surrounded him. Wilkins looked around, then up. *Got them!* A bunch of yanks hanging out of an empty top floor window, gesticulating at him wildly.

No time to waste.

The closest cadavers were in touching distance. Wilkins dropped his shoulder and ran towards the ground floor of the building his would-be saviours were sheltering inside, but was halted in his tracks by a sudden stampede of the hideous monsters coming from both his right and his left. In what seemed like less than a second, his way through was blocked by an impenetrable-looking wall of dead flesh. Same behind him now, too. And on either side. His options were rapidly reducing to none.

'Drainpipe, soldier. Now!' a deep, southern accent bellowed.

Wilkins was momentarily aware of something flying through the air above his head, way out of reach. He looked up but before he could work out what it was, a sudden flash and belly-shaking crack answered his question for him. A grenade, thrown by the GIs as a distraction. And it seemed to work, up to a point. It exploded an uncomfortably short distance behind him, sending grit, rubble and body parts flying in all directions, causing enough of a disturbance to confuse the nearest portion of the crowd at least. Wilkins knew he wouldn't get a better chance and so he charged forward again. He kicked and punched at the vicious creatures which constantly grabbed at him, closing in on him from all sides again now the effects of the temporary distraction were fading. They surged like crashing waves, and all he could do was drop below the surface and go under. He crawled along the ground, ignoring the pain in his knees and frostbitten hands, and weaving around and between the confusing mass of staggering legs until he found the wall and the cast iron drainpipe. He raised himself up and began to climb, kicking out at any of them who tried to pull him back down. Adrenalin forced his tired body to keep moving though all he wanted to do was stop. But he knew he couldn't. *Funny how so much seems to depend on me climbing up this bloody drainpipe,* he thought, feeling like he was a young lad again, shimmying up drainpipes at prep school to escape the wrath of his house master. He allowed himself the briefest of glances down into the decaying hordes looking up, and almost fell back when one of them hooked a couple of rotting fingers into the back of one of his boots. He shook himself free and kept climbing.

Halfway up.

His fingers were numb. He didn't know how much longer he'd be able to hold on for.

Keep moving.

Almost there.

Hand over hand, and he was nearly level with the soldiers at the window now. One of the yanks was hanging out precariously, gesturing for him to try and get closer. But he was more than ten feet away, and Wilkins was more than twenty feet off the ground. He didn't know how he was going to make it. Maybe he'd just have to hang here until he could hold on no longer and dropped?

The drainpipe was coming loose.

The hardware holding it in place was giving up under the strain of his considerable weight. If he didn't move fast, he knew he'd be back down amongst the dead quicker than he could say *I don't believe in Voodoo and superstitious mumbo-jumbo.*

'Use the ledge,' the American called over to him, and Wilkins looked down at his boots. It wasn't so much a ledge, more a single row of decorative bricks which jutted out slightly, but it was all he'd got. He used bullet holes and other battle damage as hand- and foot-holds and slowly began to traverse across from the drainpipe to the window.

He looked down again and wished he hadn't. There were hundreds of rotting faces looking up at him, baying for blood. His water bottle fell from his belt and he watched as it landed in the crowd and caused pandemonium. The creatures violently scrummed with each other to get it. They seemed to be miles below and still dangerously close at the same time.

'That's it,' the American said, doing what he could to keep Wilkins focused. 'You've almost done it, fella.'

With his left hand outstretched, Wilkins felt the edge of the window frame. Pressed flat against the building's pockmarked fascia, boot-tips resting on the ledge, he slowly slid himself across.

'Gotcha,' the soldier said as he dragged Wilkins inside and left him in a heap on the dusty floor. For a few seconds he couldn't move. His legs were like jelly and he had a burning in his lungs the likes of which he'd never felt before. Self-preservation took a backseat to relief. Better to be up here than down there with *them*.

His feeling of relief was tested when the first person he saw when he looked up was a Nazi, but the kraut's demeanour was such that it was clear he didn't present an immediate threat. Neither did the four Americans he could see, nor the rotund dandy who appeared more concerned with a loose thread dangling from the cuff of his jacket than anything else.

Composure returning, Wilkins remembered himself. He stood up, snapped to attention, and saluted the most senior officer he could see. 'Lieutenant Robert Wilkins. 5th Parachute Brigade.'

The weathered-looking officer returned his salute. 'Lieutenant Parker, 969th Field Artillery Battalion.'

'Pleased to make your acquaintance, Lieutenant. And thank you.'

'You're a little off the beaten track here. And all alone, too. Care to tell me what you're doing out this way?'

'Several of us were dropped in overnight. Unfortunately it seems the wind decided to deposit me over here instead of over there. I'm actually a long way off the correct beaten track, and right now I fail to see what exactly I can do about that.'

'Seems we're all stuck here together, don't it,' Lieutenant Coley said, introducing himself. 'If there is a way out of here, I'll be damned if I can see it.'

Wilkins took the opportunity to peer out through the broken window through which he'd just made his unceremonious entry. The yanks were right. There'd be no getting out of this place without a fight. Endless numbers of corpses lapped up against the base of the building like toxic waves battering the most prone lighthouse imaginable.

TRAPPED IN THE RUINS OF BASTOGNE

Gunderson was losing his patience. Forgetting himself. He was becoming increasingly aggressive towards von Boeselager who, in turn, was becoming increasingly frustrated. 'Do you really think I care? Do you think I have any remaining allegiance to the Reich after this?'

'I don't know what I think. All I know is it don't feel right you being up here with us.'

'Von Boeselager's all right. Leave him be,' Coley said. He was becoming increasingly annoyed with Gunderson's attitude, though he understood his frustration.

Gunderson stood in front of the German with his rifle primed. 'One foot out of line and I'll put a bullet between your eyes before you know it's coming.'

'Stand down, soldier,' Coley ordered.

'I can hit a dime at a hundred yards, ain't nowhere here you'll be safe.'

'I said stand down!' Coley yelled.

At that moment Lieutenant Parker returned, having taken the opportunity to relieve himself on the staircase. 'What's going on here?' he demanded.

'Just keeping an eye on the kraut,' Gunderson answered quickly.

'Good.'

'I told you,' Coley protested, 'he's all right. He saved my neck a couple a times out there.'

'You buying any of this horse shit?' Gunderson asked his commanding officer.

'You know me, Gunderson. My golden rule when it comes to trusting a kraut is to never trust a kraut.'

'Damn right,' Escobedo said from across the way. 'None of us would be in this damn mess if it wasn't for him and his kind.'

'We should kick him back out there right now,' Gunderson said, like a dog with a bone. 'Feed him to those monsters downstairs.'

'And how exactly would that help your position?' von Boeselager countered. The harshness of his accent made him sound more aggressive than he intended.

'What's he sayin'?' Escobedo demanded, addressing his question to anyone but the German.

'This gentleman wouldn't be more than a mouthful to those creatures outside,' said Wilkins. 'And just for the record, I happen to think he's right. Losing any one of us right now would be most wasteful.'

'Least he'd be gone.'

'Very true, but I think we've probably got far more to gain from working together than by using each other as bait, wouldn't you agree?'

'Don't follow...'

'Look, the one thing we know with any certainty here is that this horrific malady is German borne.'

'All the more reason to be done with him.'

'No,' Wilkins said abruptly, looking in turn at Parker, Escobedo then Gunderson. 'I believe quite the opposite, actually. Even if von Boeselager here doesn't fully understand what's happening, chances are he'll lead us to someone who does. I also happen to think he'll be more than willing to share whatever information he has with us, don't you?'

'And what if he tells us a crock of shit?'

'And what if he doesn't? Have any of you stopped to think about what's actually happening here?'

'Been too busy trying to stay alive and keep this place out of filthy Nazi hands,' Gunderson said angrily, still holding his rifle ready.

'And from what I've seen and heard, you fellows have done a commendable job in some pretty bloody awful circumstances. But I really would recommend looking a little further than the end of your nose.'

'I ain't sure I like your tone,' Lieutenant Parker said, and Lieutenant Coley stood up and positioned himself at the centre of the conversation. He wasn't sure, but he thought he'd seen the end of

Gunderson's rifle waver slightly, like the sniper thought he might be aiming at the wrong person.

'Let's dial things back a little, shall we?' Coley said, doing his best to mediate. 'We're all at the end of our tethers. We've all had to see and do things we'd rather not have since we've been over here, and this kind of abrasive attitude won't help none.'

'If I've caused offence, then I apologise,' Wilkins said.

'Apology accepted,' Coley said quickly, not affording the others any chance to prolong the argument. 'Now as it happens, I have given a lot of thought to what's happening here, and I know it ain't good. I reckon there's a storm coming.'

'You're right, Lieutenant.'

'Care to explain, Coley?' Lieutenant Parker said.

'You had much hand-to-hand with those freakish things outside?' He paused and looked around at the other men, all of them now intently staring at him. 'When we first came across those damn things, they was just krauts. Now take a look into the crowds outside and tell me what you see. There's marines out there. There's Brits. There's civilians. There's kids... do I need to go on?'

'Yeah, you do,' Gunderson grunted. 'What exactly are you sayin'?'

'That things are getting more than a little out of hand.'

Coley looked at von Boeselager, who nodded. 'He is right. I'd heard rumour that the intention was to create a serum which would lead to an army of super-soldiers. I knew nothing of the side-effects of which the lieutenant talks, though I suspect the likelihood of this happening was known at the highest levels of the Reich.'

'It's your fault, damn Nazi pig,' Escobedo spat from the corner.

'Hardly.'

'You knew about this... you knew what was going to happen.' He turned to face Parker. 'We should kill him now, Lieutenant. Throw him out for feed.'

'And what would that achieve?' Wilkins asked. 'Gentlemen, this is getting tedious. Look, I know I've not been here long, but it's been long enough to be able to see that this chap is as concerned as the rest of us. If he still had the ideals of the Third Reich at heart, do you think he'd be fighting alongside you?'

'Yeah, but—'

'But nothing,' Wilkins interrupted.

Coley was equally tired of the bickering. He raised his voice to make himself heard over the disgruntled hubbub. 'Things are getting out of hand out there. The krauts have lost control of their weapon.'

'Precisely the point I was going on to make,' Wilkins agreed.

'So if they've lost control, what happens next?' Escobedo asked.

'You have to understand that this is a weapon of such understated ferocity that its effects cannot be fully contained,' von Boeselager answered.

'You've hit the nail on the head, Jerry,' Wilkins said. 'I saw enough to confirm that in the short time I was out there among them. The creatures the germ has created are not just vicious soldiers, they're also cannibals with an insatiable thirst for blood.'

'You've been watching too many movies,' Gunderson interrupted, and he laughed nervously because he knew this wasn't fantasy, it was reality.

'I don't believe their cannibalistic intents are the most terrifying aspect of them.'

'What then?' Parker demanded.

'I found a British chap out there. A colleague of mine, as it happens. He was hanging by his parachute from a tree, tangled up with no way of easily getting himself down, just left hanging. Several of those things had attacked him.'

'And?'

'And he'd become one of them. When I found him he was in such a terrible state that it would have been impossible for him to continue to function. And yet that's exactly what he did. Still hanging from the tree, more blood spilled than was left in his body, and he still tried to attack me.'

'What point are you making, soldier?'

'That these creatures are infectious. That whatever this serum is the Nazis have developed, it remains in the infected person's body and is passed on when they attack others.'

'That's what I've seen too,' Coley said. 'And that's what scares me the most. Every single person one of those monsters out there kills goes on to become like them. And each one of them has the capacity and potential to kill more.'

'It's exponential,' Wilkins said. 'Their numbers will just keep increasing.'

'Until we get rid of them all,' Escobedo said.

'Or until they're all that's left.'

'You have to you take out the head,' Gunderson said. 'That seems to do the trick.'

'The brain is the control centre,' von Boeselager said. 'To be sure of killing them – if you can kill something which is already dead – you have to destroy the brain.'

There came an unexpectedly polite-sounding cough from the far corner of the dusty room. Henri Mercel cleared his throat to speak. The first time he'd said anything in an age. 'Monsieur... your friend in the tree, he... how you say? He was one of the *monstres horribles*?'

'Yes, he was. He'd literally not set foot on Belgian soil, so he can only have been infected as a result of the vicious attack he was subjected to.'

'Fits with everything we've seen,' Coley said.

Mercel nodded meekly but remained quiet.

'So what do we do?' Escobedo asked.

'Short of laying waste to the whole region, I'm all out of ideas,' Parker said, slumping back against the wall.

'Or getting out of here,' Gunderson suggested. 'Complete withdrawal. Let them things lay waste to each other. Tear themselves apart.'

'I'm afraid I don't think that will happen,' Wilkins said. 'From what I've observed, they'll only fight with each other if they're trying to get to one of us.'

'One of us?'

'Someone who's still alive. No, I wish it was as simple as that. War very rarely is.'

'Thanks for the words of wisdom, limey.'

'Can it, Gunderson,' Parker ordered.

Wilkins was unfazed. 'There has to be a way to stop this undead scourge. Perhaps our German friend here can enlighten us?'

'I'll enlighten him if he don't.'

'Gunderson, quit,' Lieutenant Parker warned him again.

Von Boeselager looked anxiously around the room. 'I know nothing.'

'We'll have to beat it out of him.'

'Did you not hear me? What is the point? You might as well kill me now. If I don't have any information, you'll kill me. If I did have anything, you'll beat it from me then kill me. What choice do I have?'

'None whatsoever.'

'Come on, men,' Coley said. 'Don't you get it? Those ugly bastards out there are the enemy now. So we can stop bickering and work together to try and make a difference here, or we can just beat each other to death. Whatever happens, none of us is getting out of here without the help of the others. And if you're thinking of stopping in our little crow's nest, then I reckon you'll die alone up here, starving to death as you try to avoid being eaten. And all you'll have running through your head is a whole load of questions about where this is going to end, because for what it's worth I reckon Lieutenant Wilkins here is right. This won't stop here. This is just the beginning of it. This plague of the undead will spread and it'll keep spreading.'

'My family, your family, King George, your president, your Fuhrer...' Wilkins looked around the room at each man in turn. 'A weapon has been unleashed here which respects no borders and shows no mercy. The Nazis have opened the gates of hell.'

AT THE FRONT
THE ELSENBORN RIDGE

There had been so much of a commotion in and around Bastogne that you'd have been forgiven for thinking the battle to hold the Elsenborn Ridge had gone unnoticed. Like Bastogne, the area had been key to the Germans' objective of capturing the port of Antwerp and, also like at Bastogne, here the Fuhrer's plans had been thwarted.

It had been a long and fragmented battle throughout the preceding month, but it had been a largely successful one too. The inexperienced troops of the 99th Infantry Division had initially been placed here in mid-November and had held back the Germans despite the enemy's superior firepower. The Americans had been well-prepared. They'd dug-in across this wide swathe of rugged terrain with dogged persistence and had risen to the enormous challenge presented to them. They'd been stretched to the limit – physically and emotionally – but had responded with a concentrated, coordinated and extraordinarily well-directed response which had kept Jerry on the back foot.

It was at dawn on a cold morning in late December that the final German attack on the American defensive line along the Elsenborn Ridge began. The days preceding had seen the GIs celebrating Christmas as best they could in the circumstances with wine, roast turkey, and letters and parcels from home. It was almost enough to distract a man and make him think he was somewhere other than this ice-cold, hellish place for a while.

Almost.

The Nazis came pouring out of the forest north of Rocherath, loaded up with kit and ready to depose the Americans from their positions.

Not a chance.

They were met with a volley of shells which rained down on them, and by the time the dust and smoke cleared, the fields were filled with German bodies.

There was much rejoicing in the American ranks. A small but crucial victory against all the odds. It felt like something of an analogy for the larger battles taking place in the Ardennes.

The muted celebrations in the allied ranks were short-lived.

Private Billy Bowker, a kid from Wyoming who was straight out of school and straight into battle, lifted his head from his foxhole once the noise had died down and looked around. His daddy had always said that if something seemed too easy, then the job probably wasn't finished yet. He thought that must be the case this morning. He'd taken out a couple of krauts himself with his weapon when they'd managed to get this far through the chaos but, for the most part, the shells had done all the damage.

Bowker had heard the stories, of course, and he'd talked at length to a couple of boys who'd seen and fought them first-hand, but nothing came close to the gut-wrenching fear he felt when he saw them for himself.

From his low dug-in position, to all intents and purposes the field stretching out ahead of him looked like someone had been trying to grow a crop of body parts. Hands stuck up like Jerry was asking for help. Elsewhere a truncated leg like a sapling tree, defying physics and the weather to stay standing upright. Not far away, a kraut on his back like he was lying on a beach, sunbathing. Bowker watched that one for a while, making sure he was dead. He'd have to deal with him if he wasn't.

They came out of the mist.

He knew straightaway that there was something different about these soldiers. Something about the way they moved. Ponderous at times, borderline lethargic. Exactly how you didn't want to move if you'd just witnessed a couple hundred of your comrades blown to kingdom come in this exact same spot. But still they came, and it took Bowker a while to figure out that it was *them*.

The Americans had shells enough to spare.

Another volley of mortars came from behind, flying over Bowker's head and blasting seven shades out of the frozen field and most of the approaching German soldiers. Bowker glanced up from his foxhole once again to see several of them still moving towards the American line, apparently without a damn care in the world. Curiosity kept his head up and exposed and he watched with disbelief as they continued their advance. One of them, it appeared, had been hit. A soldier dressed in off-white fatigues, one side of his body drenched with his own blood, kept coming like nothing had happened. His rifle hung useless. His right arm blown off below the elbow.

More shells, because these damn things weren't stopping for anyone.

And now gunfire.

And now men elsewhere along the Elsenborn ridge were up out of their dug-outs, shooting at the enemy unopposed. *Like shooting fish in a barrel*, he thought, but it really wasn't. They kept on coming. Whether they were shot or blown up, the damn things just kept on coming and coming. And as Bowker found to his cost, picking them off from a distance wasn't as easy as it looked. All he did was miss a couple, then got himself distracted by a couple more coming from a different angle. Then by the time he was ready to point and shoot at the first ones again, two had become four, then six, then more.

The gunner firing the 240mm Howitzer didn't even know Private Bowker was there when he hit the undead crowd.

IN THE RUINS
OF BASTOGNE

Escobedo had hoped that the night might have brought some relief. He'd thought the setting of the sun and the plunging of the outside world into darkness would render the undead masses all but invisible. Out of sight, he'd thought, and out of mind. But nothing could have been further from the truth. Though he'd initially been glad to lose sight of the sea of evil, twisted faces below, now it was what he couldn't see that scared him more. Where were they? Had they managed to get into the building? Was that really Gunderson lying next to him, or one of *them*? His mind was playing tricks. Cruel and vicious tricks.

They'd stripped some timber from the walls and put a blockade across the open window frame as best they could, and that allowed them to light a small fire in the darkest corner of the rubble-filled room in which they continued to shelter. The already low temperature had plummeted like a stone. The wind cut through them like knives. Worst of all, there was no respite from the noise. It travelled unopposed through the vacuum which was the centre of Bastogne: the relentless muffled thumps and crashes of their colleagues at the front doing all they could to defend themselves and the locals against the undead hordes.

Earlier, Wilkins had crept down to a lower floor with Lieutenant Parker to try and better assess their situation. It hadn't taken long. 'That's us screwed,' had been the lieutenant's brief but succinct assessment, and Wilkins had been hard pushed not to completely agree.

The dead still filled the square outside. Whereas earlier there had been some room for manoeuvre, now the sheer mass of them converging on this central point had begun to cause real problems. With the rest of Bastogne so desolate, they continued to be drawn to this place and now there were too many coming in for any to get out. Occasional flashes of light from distant exploding munitions revealed the full extent of the horrific scene. It reminded Wilkins of the vast crowds of revellers he'd seen in Trafalgar Square back home in London, the last New Year's Eve before the war. It chilled him to the bone to imagine this vile infection crossing the channel and spreading amongst his fellow countrymen. Being an island had frequently been to the United Kingdom's advantage. Should the Nazi germ reach British shores, however, he knew his country's geography would become a curse. Millions of diseased people trapped in a relatively confined space, transmitting the scourge to millions more until none were left untainted. It didn't bear thinking about. 'We have to do absolutely everything in our power to stop this awful disease from spreading,' he'd whispered to Lieutenant Parker.

'You ain't wrong,' Parker had replied without hesitation. 'But how can any of us expect to make a difference, man? There are thousands of these damn monsters already, and if the things you and the kraut were saying earlier are true, then it ain't gonna be long before thousands become hundreds of thousands... then millions.'

'I know, but we have to remain positive, don't we? We have to believe we can make a difference. Each one of us.'

'Granted, but if you believe you alone can change the direction of something like this, then I reckon you must have your head firmly wedged up your ass. No offence.'

'None taken, Lieutenant,' Wilkins said wryly, resolutely polite. 'But you have to remember, it's likely that one man started this whole nightmare, and I'll wager our German friend upstairs could name a particular individual who has had the most dramatic effect on world events recently, wouldn't you agree?'

'You talkin' about Adolf?'

'The one and only, thank goodness.'

The two men crept back inside and began to climb. 'I reckon we just hunker down here 'til something happens to distract them, don't you?'

'I think you're probably right. Our choices are frustratingly limited this evening.'

They soon reached the top floor, and found everyone just as they'd left them. Sitting around waiting like this didn't sit well with any soldier, irrespective of rank or side. Henri Mercel, in contrast, seemed content to do as little as possible. He'd barely spoken. Barely even moved in an age. 'What d'you reckon to that one?' Parker asked, gesturing at the overweight Belgian. He was slumped in the corner of the room, occasionally moaning and licking his lips, swallowing hard. 'Looks like he's coming down with something.'

'We should keep an eye on him,' Wilkins suggested.

'We should ditch him. Seems to me he's a dead weight. We'll have more than enough to do when we get out of this place. Don't need a no-good nobody like him slowing us down.'

Rations were pooled. Food was distributed.

The night was long and largely without rest. Wilkins and the Americans took turns watching von Boeselager and Mercel as well as keeping an eye on what was happening outside.

The first light of day was nervously beginning to creep over the shattered landscape of Bastogne when all hell broke loose on the top floor of the dilapidated building.

Henri Mercel groaned in pain. His skin was clammy, blanched white, and he was sweating profusely.

His breathing became shallow and laboured.

Then stopped.

'He dead?' Gunderson asked with his now customary lack of tact, and he prodded his belly with the barrel of his rifle.

All awake now, all watching intently. The group of soldiers became hushed. The silence was almost reverent.

Escobedo was about to get closer to the obese Belgian to check for a pulse, when Mercel opened his eyes wide and lunged at him. Escobedo instinctively grabbed the civilian's shoulders and locked his elbows to keep him at a distance, but he lost his balance and was forced down onto his back. The weight of the writhing Belgian was hard to support, but he knew he couldn't allow his snapping jaws anywhere near him. Blood-tinged drool spilled freely from his mouth, soaking and staining Escobedo's already grubby kit. 'Get this crazy bastard off me!' he hissed.

Von Boeselager obliged. He grabbed Mercel's shoulders and slammed him over onto his back, leaving Escobedo free to roll away. Mercel's gross size was an advantage to the soldiers; he was like a turtle on its shell, struggling to right his considerable bulk, thrashing his dumpy arms and legs. In the sudden melee, the madness of movement in the half-light of dawn, von Boeselager picked up a pistol that Escobedo had dropped, held it against Mercel's forehead, and fired.

'You must destroy the brain. It's the only way to be certain.'

'Thank you,' Lieutenant Parker said. He held his hand out and von Boeselager gave up the pistol. Parker gestured for him to move. 'Back over there. Keep an eye on him, Gunderson.'

Both the German and Gunderson did as ordered.

Wilkins and Coley studied the Belgian's chubby corpse for a few moments longer. Wilkins reached out to touch the dead man's face, but stopped when von Boeselager called out. 'No! Please, do not touch it. The germ is easily transmitted.'

Wilkins nodded appreciatively and then dragged the bulky body by its feet to the open window. The lighting was slightly better there. He cautiously peeled back the dead man's trouser leg to reveal a gangrenous wound near his left ankle. There were uniform, semi-circular marks around the tear in his flesh. 'Bugger me, this selfish sod had been bitten. Look! He came up here knowing full well he was already infected.'

'Get rid of him then, Lieutenant,' Lieutenant Coley said, and Wilkins obliged. He lifted Mercel's feet and flipped him out over the ledge. He watched him complete almost a full somersault before landing on his back in the crowd below with a nauseating thud.

Lieutenant Parker stared at von Boeselager. 'I still reckon he knows more than he's letting on.'

Von Boeselager remained silent. Tight-lipped. No eye contact. Staring straight ahead.

'We should beat it out of him,' Gunderson said.

No flicker of emotion from the Nazi.

'Let's not,' Wilkins suggested.

'You a sympathiser all of a sudden, 'cause he stepped up just now?' Parker asked, a surprising amount of venom in his voice.

'No, Lieutenant, I'm most definitely not.'

'What then?'

'It's clear Mr von Boeselager here wants to get out of Bastogne as much as the rest of us. We can use that to our advantage.'

'How so?'

'He can create a diversion and draw the dead away, allowing you good folks to leave in the opposite direction.'

'What makes you think he'll play ball?' Escobedo asked.

'I was about to ask the same question,' von Boeselager said.

'Because I'll go with him.'

'What?'

'You heard me. Von Boeselager and I will leave here and make enough noise to distract the dead. It makes sense if you think about it... he's certainly helped you Lieutenant Coley, and both Mr Escobedo and I were very grateful for his interjection just now. Surely he deserves better than to be frog-marched off to a POW camp?'

'You want to let a kraut walk free?' Gunderson said, not quite able to believe what he was hearing.

'No, I want to use him to let you gents walk free. How does that sound?'

'Sounds like a dumbass plan to me, sir.'

'Gotta admit, it doesn't sound like the best of deals,' Coley agreed.

'What's happened here has changed everything,' Wilkins said. 'The battle lines have been re-drawn. Our priorities have changed, both as soldiers and as men. As husbands, fathers, brothers...'

Von Boeselager took them all by surprise. 'I will do it,' he announced suddenly. 'My commanding officers, they do not understand what they have done. The Fuhrer regards what is happening here as another step towards victory. He cannot see what he has unleashed.'

'You can't make deals with a kraut,' Parker warned. 'He'll double-cross us.'

'Not *us*,' Wilkins corrected him. 'Me. I'm not asking you to take any chances.'

'Why would I double-cross anyone?' von Boeselager asked. 'You men are from the United States, thousands of miles from here. Lieutenant Wilkins, your home is safe from this disease for the moment. My family, however, is close. My wife and daughter are in Mannheim. If, as Lieutenant Wilkins and I both believe, the power and reach of the undead will continue to increase, then my family will inevitably soon pay the ultimate price. We are trained soldiers, they are not. Gertrud is barely four years old. If men like us cannot beat these creatures, what hope is there for my little girl?'

He stopped talking momentarily, his eyes damp with tears, and looked around at the faces which watched him intently.

'Yeah, I got a kid too,' Escobedo said. 'Name's Joey. About the same age as your kid by the sounds of things. Cuts me up not knowing where he is or even if he's safe.'

Lieutenant Coley moved closer to the German and put his hand on his shoulder. 'I trust this guy,' he announced. He looked straight at him. 'Talk, Erwin. If you know anything you haven't told us yet, talk.'

Von Boeselager took a deep breath. 'The serum was created by scientists at the Polonezköy camp in Poland. Their brief was to create an unstoppable super-soldier, but they were only partially successful. There were two strands to their research, as I understand: prolonging life and increasing strength and ferocity. As you can see from the crowd outside this building, they succeeded to an extent, but at the expense of control.'

'You're not telling us nothing we don't already know,' Lieutenant Parker said.

Von Boeselager ignored him. 'With the surprise attack in this region already being planned, our leaders ignored the scientists' concerns and deployed the serum in its current unstable form while their research continued. In fact, I understand that one of the scientist's reservations resulted in him being removed from the project altogether. He is being held at the concentration camp.'

'What reservations did he express?' Wilkins asked.

'The contagious aspect of the condition. He warned that it would inevitably get out of control if the infection was released into the wild.'

'And it has.'

'That has certainly proved to be the case.'

'Wait, wait, wait...' Gunderson interrupted. 'Let's slow down a second here. This guy's doing a heck of a lot of talking, but he ain't saying much. You're making it sound like there's nothing can be done about this whole damn mess you've made, Fritz.'

'I didn't say that. There is...'

Von Boeselager stopped himself.

'What?' Parker said, aiming a pistol directly into the German's face.

'I've said enough.'

Parker was ready to fire. Wilkins positioned himself between the two of them. 'Wait.'

'He's stringing us along...'

'I don't believe so. Herr von Boeselager is a clever man.'

'We should feed him to the dead,' Gunderson suggested.

'And what would that achieve exactly? No, gentlemen, our German friend is giving us a master-class in negotiation. His knowledge is his bargaining chip.'

'If he even has any knowledge. Who says he ain't just stringing us along?'

'That's a chance I have to take.'

'Lieutenant Wilkins is right. If I told you everything I know now, there would be no reason for you to keep me alive.'

'I can't see there's much reason to do that anyway,' Gunderson said.

'I just want to get out of here and go home,' von Boeselager said. 'I want to get back to my family and see them before it is too late.'

'And if we agree and you and I leave here today?' Wilkins asked.

'Then I'll tell you everything I know. I swear.'

OUTSIDE IN THE RUINS

In a small walled courtyard behind the building in which they'd spent much of the last twenty-four hours, Wilkins, Parker and Gunderson had managed to find a safe pocket of space to explore, protected from the hordes of the dead by rubble and ruin. Wilkins uncovered a BBA035 motorcycle. It looked to have sustained only superficial damage. 'Start it up, give it a blast,' Parker suggested, but Wilkins declined. They spoke in hushed whispers.

'What, and ruin the surprise? No, thank you. I'll wait until we're ready to leave.'

'And if it doesn't start?'

'Then von Boeselager and I will be running.'

'Quite a chance you're taking.'

'Less of a chance than if I was to start the engine here and now. I'll wager the dead would find a way to pour through every available crack and crevice to get to us. Remember, wiping us out and adding to their ranks is all they're interested in. It's their very reason for existing. We'd all do well not to forget that.'

'Don't think I could forget it. I think about it every time I look at one of the damn things.'

A few minutes more work and Wilkins was ready. Gunderson – something of a grease-monkey – had checked the bike over as best he could and given it as clean a bill of health as possible given the circumstances. While he'd worked, Parker and Wilkins had cleared enough debris from an area of ground to enable the bike to be ridden out of this safe space. They'd placed a number of timber joists next to each other and rested them against the top of what had originally been a five foot brick wall, creating a makeshift exit ramp.

Done.

Time to move.

Wilkins leant back into the building and gave a thumbs-up to Coley who was watching from the top of the stairs. He, in turn, gave Escobedo the word, then escorted von Boeselager down to ground level. Wilkins gestured for the German to take the controls of the bike. 'The hell are you doing, soldier?' Parker asked. 'You're letting the kraut drive? You must be as stupid as Gunderson here looks.'

Gunderson grunted in disgust.

'We're both about to risk our lives out there, Lieutenant. I have to trust him, and he has to trust me. Otherwise neither of us are going to last long, are we?'

'Don't reckon you're going to last long anyway, in all honesty.'

'For all our sakes I hope we do. Now can we get things moving please?'

Parker nodded.

Coley shook von Boeselager's hand. 'Thank you. Good luck.'

'You too, Lieutenant.'

Wilkins sat on the back of the bike and wrapped his arms around the German's waist. High above them, Escobedo hung precariously out of the top floor window looking down. When he saw they were ready, he pulled the pin from a grenade and hurled it as far as he could across the packed square. Then another.

Two loud blasts in quick succession. Wilkins felt them travel up through his feet and into his belly.

One more grenade. Their meagre stock was being rapidly emptied.

Another explosion, then a deep, growling, thunderous noise as what was left of a café collapsed in on itself like a house of cards.

'Do it,' Wilkins ordered.

'This is madness.'

'I know. Fun, isn't it?'

Von Boeselager kick-started the bike, and on the third attempt it roared into life. He rocked back, then powered forward, straight up the low ramp they'd built, and over the top of the wall.

If the grenades didn't distract them, thought Wilkins, *then we're dead men.*

The bike crashed down into an area of relative space on the fringes of the crowd, the suspension almost giving out under the weight but just about holding up. The back wheel threatened to kick out from under them, but von Boeselager instinctively hung out the other way to compensate, then swung back and accelerated hard.

The plan appeared to be working. When Wilkins looked up (he'd initially had his eyes shut and his head down) he saw that the explosions and the crumbling building had, mercifully, distracted many of the hundreds of rabid corpses which had continued to swarm here in the town square. It had left this side of the square – the area through which he and von Boeselager now rode at speed – relatively clear. Those members of the massive dead army which were interested more by the bike than the bang now found that they couldn't get through. With half the rotting crowd trying to go in one direction and the rest of them the other, very few of the corpses were actually going anywhere.

Von Boeselager accelerated again, weaving this way and that, still nowhere near sure they were going to make it.

From his high vantage point Escobedo watched the motorcycle race away. The two men were out of sight in seconds, but the engine of the bike could still be heard minutes later. And, to his selfish delight, he noticed that their noise seemed to be of incredible interest to hordes of the dead. Sections of the vast rotting crowd had begun to move *en masse*, fruitlessly chasing after them.

The soldier ran down to the others who were waiting for him in the rubble downstairs.

'This gonna work?' asked Lieutenant Coley.

'We'll soon find out,' Lieutenant Parker replied.

Their escape route had been planned, both in terms of getting away from the immediate area and getting out of Bastogne and on to Assenois. Working quickly and quietly, Parker and Gunderson scaled a wall then reached back for the others and their supplies. It took little more than a couple of minutes to complete the evacuation. Coley cleared a few undead stragglers out of their way. One of them came hard at him, but a fist to the face followed by a bowie knife between the eyes dealt with the threat.

Gunderson went for another one of the creatures, but Parker held him back. The dead woman was walking away from them, hypnotised like so many others by a combination of the ruins of the collapsed café building and the distant whine of the disappearing motorbike.

'We good?' Lieutenant Parker asked, looking around at the others. He didn't need to wait for an answer. He knew that they were.

ESCAPE

The motorcycle raced out of Bastogne. Wilkins held onto von Boeselager for dear life. The German struggled to stay focussed, such was the number of horrific sights they witnessed as they sped away from the town and out through the Belgian countryside. A Mark V Panther blocked the road and von Boeselager had to swerve around to avoid its stationary cannon. The tank was as dead as its crew. Just one soldier was moving. White suit, cold flesh... he reached out for the bike as it powered past but could only grab at the warm air it left in its wake.

The dead were somewhat fewer in number out here, though they were never far. Wilkins had naively hoped that because the town had been so heavily clogged by these despicable creatures, the countryside might be relatively clear. How wrong he'd been. Von Boeselager lost control of the bike when the front tyre sank into a pothole which had been hidden by snow, and despite his best efforts, he and Wilkins were sent skidding along the track. Von Boeselager immediately saw to the bike, leaving Wilkins to defend their position because a swarm was already nearing. He used his clasp knife to dispatch several of them until the German had righted the machine and was ready to leave. Wilkins, who was grappling with a particularly noxious foe, put a bullet between the dead man's eyes then shoved the lifeless corpse away.

'Behind you!' von Boeselager shouted, and Wilkins span around to see another hideous cadaver coming at him at speed. The creature was close enough for its outstretched fingertips to brush Wilkins' tunic. He kicked the monster away and ran for the bike.

'Just go!' he shouted, and as the bike began to move, Wilkins looked back over his shoulder, his heart thumping, at the place they'd just been. The dead were crawling out from between the trees in ever-increasing numbers. It was almost as if the forest was alive.

Mile after mile, Von Boeselager struggled to balance speed with safety. If anything, he drove too slowly, not wanting to risk losing control again. Last time they'd been lucky, but they both knew luck was in short supply these days.

A fork in the road.

To the right, the fighting at the front. To the left, everything else. Wilkins still gripped his pistol and wondered whether he'd need to use it or whether von Boeselager would continue to play ball. He was relieved when the German asked, 'which way?'

'By my reckoning I need to travel another two miles west.'

'West? But that's back towards the fighting.'

'I know.'

Von Boeselager was distracted. More dead soldiers were approaching. Gnarled faces and twisted bodies. 'We need to move.'

'What's your first name?'

'What? Now is not the time for this.'

'I don't think I'll see you again, old chap.'

'Erwin. My name is Erwin.'

'Pleased to have met you, Erwin. I'm Robert.'

'And have you gone quite mad, Robert?'

'Not at all, my friend. I just thought it was important for us to part as men, not soldiers.'

The dead were nearing.

'You want to part here? We must keep moving.'

'We need to go our separate ways. We both have important missions ahead of us. Yours is to return to your family and keep them safe. Mine, I'm afraid, is a little more onerous.'

'I don't understand.'

'And that's probably for the best.'

Wilkins dismounted. Von Boeselager looked at him with incredulity. 'What are you doing?'

'My duty,' Wilkins replied, and he stepped to one side and fired a single well-aimed shot which brought down the nearest corpse.

The sound of the motorcycle's engine was like a call to the faithful. As they'd both expected, the periphery was alive with movement now.

'Go,' Wilkins said. 'I'll be fine from here. Thank you.'

Von Boeselager paused, clearly unsure. 'Wait... before we part...'

'What?'

'The camp I told you about... the scientists responsible for this nightmare...'

'What about them?'

'One was Swedish, the other from the *Vaterland*.'

'And?'

'And I was told that the Swede realised the full implications of the work he was being ordered to do, and he rebelled. That's why they continue to hold him in Polonezköy.'

'And the German?'

'I have already explained. He was taken back to Berlin to complete his work to create a super-soldier with the strength of the monsters we've seen, but with more control and consideration.'

'That doesn't bear thinking about,' Wilkins said, and he broke away momentarily to take care of the next nearest cadaver.

'The Swede was trying to develop something that would stop the condition from progressing...'

'An inhibitor? That would make sense. It's the only option, I guess. A cure would be out of the question. How can you cure something that's already dead?'

'Quite.'

'It is not much but I have told you everything I know, I am afraid. Do you believe me?'

Wilkins thought for a moment. 'I believe I do. We want the same thing, you and I.'

There were seven corpses closing in now. Several were moving with increased speed. Wilkins holstered his pistol.

'Go,' he said. 'Get out of here. Get home and do what you need to do.'

'But I cannot leave you out here like this...'

'I'll be fine. Now go! Find your family!'

And with that Wilkins turned and ran along the road that stretched deeper into the forest. Von Boeselager roared away in the opposite direction.

The dead were everywhere. He could sense them. *Feel* them. Fortunately, as he'd found previously, by slowing down and mimicking their often clumsy and ponderous movements, he was able temporarily to fool them into thinking he was just another of their number. Mostly. Through bad luck he rounded the broad trunk of an ancient Norwegian Spruce at the exact same time a disfigured Nazi corpse came the other way. The dead soldier's reactions were guttural, his speed surprising but no match for Wilkins. By the time the creature had opened its jaws, yellowed teeth ready to clamp down and rip the British man's flesh from his bones, Wilkins had already struck. He plunged the blade of his clasp knife into the dead man's temple, and his artificially prolonged life was ended instantly. He fell to the ground with the grace of a sack of potatoes. Wilkins wiped his blade on his trousers then moved on.

He checked his map and compass again in the eerie half-light of the forest, taking care not to draw any more unwanted attention than was necessary. The sun was all but hidden behind a layer of impenetrable grey cloud which was, in turn, hidden by the tree canopy overhead. If his calculations were accurate and his bearings were right, he'd reach the road to Liege soon enough, and from there he'd head west to the village. He was moving in the right direction, he was sure he was, but it didn't take much to ignite his nagging self-doubts today. Here he was, completely alone in a war-torn, foreign land, swarming with an unnatural enemy, with his sweetheart hundreds and hundreds of miles away and what felt like the weight of the world on his shoulders. Things couldn't get much worse.

Or could they?

He froze when he heard more sounds of movement nearby. More corpses? The noise was initially directionless, confused by the dense mass of trees. The camouflage they provided was welcome, but the way they diffracted the light and sound was not. He pressed himself up against another trunk and peered around, trying to see without being seen, ready to repel the next vicious attack.

A Nazi patrol.

He could tell from the way they were moving that the figures up ahead were human. Constant noises were audible now over the soldiers' bluster – the engines of several jeeps, weapons being readied, orders being shouted. From the little he could make out, these men seemed to be retreating back from the front. He tried to believe it was the allies forcing them back, but he knew it almost certainly wouldn't be.

Wilkins held his position – uncomfortably close – and watched as the increasingly frenzied movement continued. He heard voices yelling. '*Schnell, schnell! Holen sie sich das haubitze in Position!*'

It looked like they were the remnants of one of the Volksartilleriekorps. Field reports Wilkins had heard had intimated that they'd proved to be ill-equipped and had been left behind as the German front had advanced as part of Hitler's surprise offensive across the Ardennes.

'*Schnell! Die monster kommen!*'

Wilkins couldn't risk going backwards or forwards, and instead he went up. He swiftly hauled himself up into the branches of the first tree he found with boughs low enough and strong enough to support his weight. He hugged the trunk of a tired old oak for all he was worth. A distinctly British tree in unfamiliar surroundings. Memories of home gave him the slightest crumb of comfort. And in the same way this lone oak stood proud amongst the spruce, he quickly realised how his survival out here was due in no small part to the fact he was on his own. The old adage of there being safety in numbers usually held true, but not today.

From his precarious perch, Wilkins watched another bloody battle quickly unfold. The Nazis, he deduced, had indeed been retreating, for their actions appeared frantic and uncoordinated; not cold, ruthless and clinical as he'd come to expect from the enemy. The ragtag convoy moved through the forest, but then ground to a halt when a stormtrooper lookout spotted that they were running towards as many ghouls as they were running from. Caught out by the openness of this part of the wood, they had been all but surrounded and their noise was doing nothing to help hide their position.

The Germans began to dig in, ready for the inevitable.

Wilkins was distracted by the movement of more of the dead near the base of the tree in which he was hiding. They were moving in a pack, almost in formation, and for a moment his heart leapt. They were allied troops. Americans, by the looks of things. He felt a momentary surge of relief when he recognised their uniforms, then utter despair.

Dead.

All of them.

But still fighting.

There must have been almost thirty of them all told, maybe half as many again. They came towards the German position with a chilling lack of fear, advancing with almost arrogant slowness.

'*Feuer!*'

A howitzer was fired into the advancing undead at close range. Wilkins tasted bile at the back of his throat as bodies were blown to pieces, a smoky haze of gore and dismembered limbs sent flying in all directions. Trees and fauna exploded outwards. A disembodied head landed in the leaf-litter and burst like an over-ripe melon. Wilkins gagged and forced himself to look up, not down.

He peered around the side of his tree – still standing, thankfully – and witnessed several members of the Volksartilleriekorps desperately trying to regroup and reload, but they were far too slow and far too late. They concentrated their fire on the dead coming at them from ahead, but there were twice as many more approaching from behind. The undead army surged through and left no survivors in their wake.

Several of the few remaining Germans began to run, scarpering in all directions. One of them, a young lad with an unruly mop of white-blond hair, tripped and fell over the roots of the tree in which Wilkins was hiding. He rolled onto his back and looked up. Sworn enemies caught sight of each other, but their uniformed distinctions were immediately forgotten. Wilkins felt genuinely sorry for the kraut. His face was streaked with tears. Wide-eyed and helpless, he didn't look old enough to be fighting. '*Hilf mir. Bitte...*'

Before Wilkins could react, two dead Americans grabbed the boy and killed him with brutal savagery. The expressions on the dead soldiers' faces chilled him to the core. No flicker of emotion. Relentless. Remorseless. One of them dug deep into the German's exposed torso and pulled out a handful of steaming, bloody innards. The soldier was still alive as he was eviscerated. He screamed with pain as his insides were emptied out like streamers.

The all-conquering wave of dead figures continued through the forest, heading after the handful of Nazis who'd somehow managed to evade them. Wilkins held his breath so as not to make the slightest sound, and prayed they'd pass him by unnoticed.

It was more than an hour before the last of the undead had disappeared from view.

Wilkins crept through the forest as quickly as he dared, balancing speed with the need to stay alive. The dead seemed to always be close: he'd evade one cluster, only to find himself heading straight for another. He was desperate to reach Liege, but still wasn't completely sure that he was heading in the right direction. The longer he was out here, the more his cancerous self-doubt grew. He was tired, living on his nerves... and now the already dull light in this heavily forested area was beginning to fade.

And then, finally, after hours alone, he saw it. An inconspicuous-looking cottage. Isolated. Unkempt and shabby. Its dilapidation was hidden by a light covering of snow which was continuing to fall. He checked over his shoulder, conscious that his footprints were visible and would lead straight to him. He walked on for a short while longer then doubled-back on himself in a half-hearted attempt to throw anyone who was following him off-guard.

Back at the front of the cottage again now, he knocked the door. She took a long time to answer. Too long. He thought she'd gone and cleared out and that he'd be stuck out here tonight with just the dead for company. She eventually opened the door and scowled at him, the yellow light from her oil lamp making her appear haggard, even older than her clearly advanced years. She screwed up her face to get a better look at him. '*Quelle?*'

'Madam Van Pruisen?'

'*Quelle?*' she barked at him again.

'*Savez-vous à quelle heure le départ du train du village voisin?*'

His French pronunciation was less than perfect, but it was adequate. Wilkins didn't care what time the train was leaving. Heck, he didn't even know if there *was* a train here at all. He wasn't interested in the next village, and Madam Van Pruisen knew it. At his mention of the designated phrase she roughly grabbed the collar of his tunic and pulled him inside, checking the road in either direction – both for the living and the dead – then shut and bolted the door behind him.

'*Merci madame,*' he started to say, but she wasn't interested.

'*Il est sous le lit dan la chambre à l'étage. Être rapide. Vous risquez de ma vie en étant ici.*'

'*Oui.*'

'*Vive le résistance,*' she mumbled, almost sarcastically.

He climbed the creaking staircase she pushed him towards. His translation of her words might not have been expert, but the intent of what she'd said was clear. Madam Van Pruisen was in collusion with British Intelligence, and for that he was eternally grateful. The risks she took were equal to, if not greater than, his own. He knew exactly what Jerry would do to her if they found him here.

Wilkins found the radio exactly where she said it would be, and did what he had to do.

Within minutes he was back out in the freezing cold, exposed and vulnerable again. But it didn't matter. He knew that soon, God willing, he'd be on his way back to Blighty.

AT THE FRONT
EN ROUTE FROM BASTOGNE

Lieutenants Parker and Coley, along with Gunderson and Escobedo, had escaped Bastogne by the skin of their teeth. Swarms of dead civilians and soldiers pursued them through the ruins and out into the surrounding countryside, but had been distracted *en masse* by another engagement further north. It must have been a big fight, Coley thought to himself. He could feel the detonations shaking the ground they moved over, felt the dull roar of battle in his belly.

It was cold and unforgiving out here, enough to make Escobedo almost wish he was back in Bastogne again in their hideout on high, shielded from the wind. 'Reckon we should hole up somewhere soon, sirs? Can't feel my feet...'

'Quit complaining, Escobedo,' Parker told him.

Coley held his arm up to stop them all. 'Movement. In the trees due east,' he hissed. It didn't look like much – no more than a couple of men at most – but they weren't about to take any chances. 'You and Gunderson follow the tree-line,' he said to

Parker. 'Me and Escobedo will loop round through the forest, try and come up from behind them.'

Parker nodded. He held way back with Gunderson then moved slowly forward, giving the other pair time to take up position.

The closer they got, the less concerned they were of attack. There was a jeep wedged up against the upended root of a recently felled tree. And the movement Coley had seen from a distance? It looked like there was a man down. An American at that. Coley ran to his fellow serviceman's aid, but pulled up fast. The poor bastard wasn't lying on the ground alongside the jeep, he was under it. His pelvis had been crushed under its wheels and it was clear that he'd been deliberately mowed down. He'd been there a while (they could tell from the dried blood and his unnatural pallor) but when he became aware of the others approaching, the trapped GI began to thrash furiously.

Gunderson took him out with a knife to the back of his head, affording him what little dignity he could.

The jeep – once they'd disentangled it from the tree roots and the remains of the American soldier – gave them an unexpected boost. The area of countryside through which they travelled was quiet. There was a moment of concern when they spied the outline of a Panzer up ahead, but it was a wreck. Burned out and full of corpses.

They came across another couple of GIs on the road to the front. They looked exhausted and beaten; barely able to keep their heads up, it seemed to take all the effort they could muster for them to just keep breathing and keep moving. 'Give you boys a lift somewhere?' Lieutenant Parker asked as they drew level.

'Much appreciated, sir,' the older of the two replied. 'Guess we're all heading in the same direction. I'm Hooper, and this here is Stacey. Stacey don't say much at the moment. He's seen too much if you ask me. Though I'm guessing we probably all have by now.'

'Hop in,' said Parker, and they did. Escobedo hung off the back of the jeep, allowing Hooper and Stacey to sit, squeezed up alongside Gunderson's bulk.

For half an hour or more the drive was deceptively peaceful. Six men, none of them with much to say to the others, grateful for a little rest and relaxation before the inevitable onslaught. Conversation was sparse. It was just good to have a little headspace. They all knew it wouldn't last long.

Frost and snow obscured much of the things they knew were there but didn't want to see. Bodies frozen solid were all but hidden in drifts. The wreck of an overturned Howitzer looked almost like a piece of sculpted ice in the fading light.

They heard the front before they saw it. Smelt it. Felt it, even.

The jeep was dumped when it ran out of fuel, leaving them with a short march to the battle-lines. The chaos and killing they'd briefly escaped, the destruction and devastation, the pain and suffering... all returned in a heartbeat.

Wave after wave after wave of the undead.

Fearless.

Unstoppable.

Tens of thousands of them.

The chatter in the ranks was rife:

'There ain't barely anything left of the 106th.'

'I heard they was attacking us ten to a man out west. Those damn things were fighting with each other to get a piece of our boys.'

'There was a whole host of them trapped under the Sherman, and they were still trying to come at us.'

'I ain't never seen so many krauts in one place, and all of them were coming at us. Don't know how the hell we got out of there alive. Plenty of guys didn't.'

Coley stopped by the stores to refresh and reload, then headed back out to war.

POCKLINGTON HALL NEAR LEICESTER, UNITED KINGDOM

When Isambard Gray, seventh Earl of Pocklington, had commissioned the building of this extravagant stately home in the mid-eighteen-hundreds, he could hardly have envisaged what he'd find there today. His grand yet idyllic country retreat, constructed well off the beaten track, was alive with activity. The grounds of the manor, beautifully tended and immaculately coiffured during peacetime, were now fulfilling a far more practical purpose. Several of the vast lawns had been dug over for the cultivation of vegetables on an almost industrial scale. Others now resembled great tented villages; makeshift barracks and temporary field hospitals and training grounds. There were aircraft and other military vehicles hidden in the shadows, draped with tarpaulins which, every so often, would be hurriedly pulled back to allow a swift launch from an improvised airfield. A squad of new recruits jogged through the middle of the organised chaos in their mid-splattered

PE kit; shirt and shorts, pale white legs redraw with cold.

Wilkins had mixed feelings whenever he returned here. It was good to be back in England, that much was certain, but Pocklington Hall was only ever a staging point – a place where he was debriefed, then re-briefed (although he'd already been questioned at length by a fellow agent on the way here). It was hard at times, but everyone had to do their bit. Wilkins forced himself to focus on the end-game to keep him going. He imagined a future time when this damn war would be over. A future he could share with Jocelyn. Maybe they'd settle down somewhere and bring up a couple of children together. Strange that such a seemingly normal plan felt out of reach today, like a naïve fantasy. There was much work to be done before then. Many mountains to climb. It was also funny, he thought, how nervous he felt when he knew Jocelyn was near. More anxious, sometimes, than when he'd been in battle.

The jeep he'd been travelling in for the last hour or so was a tired old jalopy. Damn noisy, too. The track along which they were now driving was pot-holed and uneven, worn away as a result of the heavy military equipment which had been dragged up and down here so many times in recent months. The din and his nerves and his lack of sleep combined to leave him feeling uncomfortably nauseous. What he'd have given for a few more hours sleep before having to face the colonel. There was little chance he'd get even another five minutes shuteye today.

The winter morning sun was beginning to climb over the treeline, bathing the English countryside in a warm yellow-orange glow, long shadows stretching. The jeep came to an abrupt halt outside the ornate entrance to the manor house, wheels crunching in gravel. The driver – Teddy Jones, an unfailingly cheerful Brummie chap – let him out. Wilkins looked to see if he could risk disappearing around the back of the building for a quick cigarette first, but no such luck. Wilberforce, that lily-livered fool, was already waiting for him at the top of the steps. 'Wilkins,' he shouted down. 'Good to see you, old boy. The colonel's waiting.'

'Now there's a surprise,' Wilkins mumbled as he smoothed his hair then brushed dirt from his sleeve before begrudgingly saluting. 'And how's the war been treating you, Wilberforce? Not caught any enemy troops hiding in your filing cabinet?'

'Ease off, old boy. Not my fault I've got a dicky ticker. Now let's not dawdle, you know what Colonel Adams is like if he's kept waiting.'

'Quite.'

Wilkins overtook Wilberforce and marched through the manor. He'd no time for the nervous, cowardly little man. *That speck of Belgian mud I've just flicked from my sleeve has seen more action than you*, he thought but didn't say. Wilberforce, an infuriating pen-pusher, was a mummy's boy. And when mummy was as well-connected socially as Lady Brenda Wilberforce, getting yourself diagnosed with a plausible medical excuse so you could stay safe in middle-England, far from the front line, was a cinch.

The manor was heaving with people. A veritable hive of activity. A grand, wide, sweeping oak-carved staircase went up, but Wilkins and Wilberforce went down, taking a dingier and far narrower staircase tucked away in one corner instead. At the foot of the stairs was a grey metal door, guarded on either side. Two stony-faced privates saluted and stepped aside, one of them opening the door to allow the officers through.

For all that was happening above ground level, there seemed to be ten-times that activity unfolding underground. The space below the manor house was immense: a vast, cavernous room filled with the low chatter of hundreds of people hard at work. Artificial yellow light barely filled the place, the fug of cigarette smoke limiting visibility even further.

In the very centre of the room, under the largest, brightest light, was a table-top map of the unfolding war in Europe. Several Wrens pushed markers representing troops, tanks and supplies around the map, informed by others with notes taken from the most recent radioed reports from around the world. Wilkins' attention was automatically drawn to the area around the Ardennes. The German offensive was marked out in a large bulge coming from the east. The allies clearly had a huge task ahead of them. As well as the Nazi army, they were also having to contend with the ever-increasing forces of the undead, which were represented on the map by the same model tanks and soldiers, daubed with bright yellow paint. Wilkins found it disconcerting just how much yellow paint he could see. It wouldn't be long before there was more yellow than anything.

Colonel Adams' distinctive, bellicose voice boomed across the operations room. 'Lieutenant Wilkins.'

Wilkins turned and saluted the colonel, then followed him into his office.

No time for niceties. 'Shut the door,' the colonel ordered.

'Yes, sir,' Wilberforce said.

'And do me a favour, Wilberforce?'

'Of course, sir.'

'Be on the other side of it when it closes, there's a good chap.'

'Yes, sir,' Wilberforce said again, sounding crestfallen, and he obediently shut himself out.

'I really can't abide that man,' the colonel said. He gestured for Wilkins to sit down on a desperately uncomfortable wooden chair, then poured him a tumbler of whiskey and slid it across the desk.

'It's a little early, Colonel.'

'Believe me, it's not. Drink.'

Rather than sit down, the colonel instead perched on the corner of his desk and looked down on Wilkins with the intensity of a displeased schoolmaster. There was a brief, awkward silence which the colonel quickly ended. 'Well? Are you just going to sit there all day, Wilkins, or are you going to give me your assessment of what you saw out there?'

'I'm sorry, sir,' he said. 'It's all been a bit of a blur.' And he knocked back his whiskey in one.

'I'm sure it has, but things are going to get a damn sight worse if we don't take action. Now tell me, are things out there really as bad as I'm being led to believe.'

'No, sir, they're worse. Much worse.'

'How so?'

'This new foe we're facing is like no other. They are already dead. This makes them both fearless and largely indestructible. And when people are killed by this unearthly new enemy, regardless of which side they were originally batting for, they all turn.'

The colonel thought for a moment and poured himself another drink. 'I'd already heard as much. You've been on the ground though, Wilkins. I want your fullest and frankest assessment of the situation.'

'It's grim, sir. Getting worse by the day. By the hour, actually.'

'And how do you see things panning out?'

'I'm no strategist and I—'

'What's your gut feeling, Lieutenant?'

'Follow the logic of this scenario through, Colonel.'

'Logic?'

'Quite. But consider the facts. The dead have extraordinary resilience and aggression and the curse which has blighted them is contagious. There will inevitably come a point when they outnumber the living.'

'That's what I feared.'

'I foresee there being a tipping point, perhaps not too far away, when the living become the minority. Then, eventually, we'll disappear altogether.'

The colonel knocked back his second drink. 'Damn those bloody Nazis,' he yelled, and he thumped his fist down onto the desk, filling the small office with noise.

'It's not completely hopeless, sir.'

'It certainly sounds that way.'

'You've heard about Polonezköy? The camp where the germ at the source of this outbreak was developed.'

'I've read the report.'

'Then you'll also know one of the scientists responsible is imprisoned there.'

'Yes, and since we received your intelligence we've been able to confirm he hasn't left the camp. In fact, no one's entered or left the camp in some time, by all accounts.'

'It strikes me that scientist is our best hope. Perhaps our only hope.'

'I completely agree, Wilkins. You leave at midnight.'

'Sir?'

'You heard me. Come on, man, did you really think I could send anyone else? You've experience of dealing with these ghouls first-hand.'

'But sir, I do think there are other men who are better equipped to—'

'Dammit, Wilkins, you're going and that's all there is to it. You wouldn't have been my first choice, granted, but as of this morning you're just about my only choice. There may have been better men, braver men, but...'

'Sir?'

'But they're dead. Some of them dead twice over. Only two of you made it back, and you're the only one still alive. I need you to accompany the team heading for Polonezköy. The fate of our country is at stake here.'

Wilkins stood up slowly, his body weighed down with fatigue and resignation. He was about to leave but he stopped, concerned by something the colonel had said. 'Two of us made it back?'

'What?'

'You said two of us made it back. Who was the other?'

'Raymond Mills. Good chap.'

'I know him. Where is he?'

The colonel paused, and Wilkins began to feel increasingly uneasy. He wasn't being told the whole story here, that much was clear. Colonel Adams picked up on his uncertainty. 'Come with me.'

Another staircase leading even farther down, deep below Pocklington Hall. Another guarded door in a place where there shouldn't have been a door at all. The guard saluted and stood aside.

On the other side of the door, a well-lit room. Small and square, no more than four yards wide and long. At the far end, a hastily-built ante-room. No door. A metal grille two bricks wide by three high. 'Get me some light in there,' the colonel ordered. A switch was flicked, and Wilkins peered inside.

Raymond Mills was dead. His uniform torn to shreds, his exposed skin equally damaged. His face was a hideous shadow of the man Wilkins remembered: a cruel caricature of a once brave and proud soldier. Mills' eyes were at once completely devoid of emotion yet full of anger and hate. When he saw Wilkins and the colonel on the other side of the grille, he threw himself at them and began to fight viciously and pointlessly, trying to get at them.

'Good God,' Wilkins said.

'Poor bastard. He was caught by one of those things just as he was getting on the plane, but by all accounts no one noticed until it was too late.'

Wilkins' mind was racing. How had they managed to get the infected officer down here? Had anyone else come into contact with him? 'You have to get rid of him, sir. Burn him, I suggest. It's necessary to bludgeon the head first to incapacitate him, then burn what's left to be sure the infection can't be spread.'

'It's perfectly safe, Wilkins. We've had our best men dealing with him. There's no way he can escape.'

'Then what's the point of keeping him in this pitiful state?'

'To study. You're a decent soldier, but you're no scientist. Our chaps tell me they need to see one of these things close-up to work out what we're dealing with. Mills fell into our lap at just the right moment.'

'There is no right moment...'

'I understand your concern, but there's no way out. He's bricked in, for goodness sake.'

'And how did you keep him restrained while the brickwork was complete?' Wilkins asked.

'He was shackled to the wall.'

'Well he's not now,' he observed as his dead colleague threw himself at the metal grille again.

'No, there was an incident with his right hand, I believe. But he is completely trapped. He doesn't have the strength to break through brick walls.'

'What kind of incident?'

The colonel seemed reluctant. 'He chewed through his own wrist to get free.'

'Christ... And you expect me to believe he won't get out? Have you stopped to consider the implications? Just by having him here you've introduced the germ to England. If he should get lose then we're all done for...'

'He *won't* get out,' Colonel Adams said, his tone increasingly short. 'My people know what they're doing here, Wilkins, and I'll have nothing bad said of them. They'll do what's asked of them and all I expect of you is that you follow your orders, and those orders are to break into Polonezköy camp, find this bloody scientist, get him out of there and deliver him to us alive. Is that clear?'

'Perfectly.'

'Glad to hear it. Now get yourself some food and some rest. You don't have long.'

'Sir.'

'There's a hell of a lot riding on this mission, Wilkins. Far more than you probably appreciate.'

IN THE GROUNDS OF POCKLINGTON HALL
MIDDAY

Despite his utter exhaustion, sleep hadn't come easily to Wilkins. Nervousness kept him awake for much of the morning. That and the constant noise and activity in and around the manor house. He admitted defeat just before lunchtime. He emerged from the room where they'd left him in a makeshift (and bloody uncomfortable) cot, and left the building through a large glass door which opened out onto a raised courtyard area. The room he'd been resting in had originally been a ballroom, though he thought it had probably been a long time since there'd been any kind of jollities to be had here. Times past this grand house would have been alive with a different kind of activity every day: socialising and drinking, dancing and swinging, all without a damn care in the world. Wilkins leant against the stone balustrade and lit a cigarette, flicking the spent match into an ornamental fish pond below, wondering if there would ever be a return to such carefree, innocent times.

'They told me you were sleeping,' she said.

He froze when he heard her voice. Didn't want to turn around in case he was dreaming or if it was a cruel trick his sleep-starved brain was playing on him.

But it wasn't.

It was her.

He turned around and saw her watching him. She looked every inch as beautiful as he remembered. Even in her Wrens uniform and with little make-up and her hair unkempt she was stunning. He ran over and grabbed hold of her. The two of them embraced, neither wanting to ever let go of the other. Their lips met with unbridled passion.

'I've missed you,' he whispered when they finally parted.

'And I missed you too, Robert. It's such a relief to see you again.'

They kissed again, but this time Jocelyn pulled away slightly. 'What's wrong?' he asked.

'I heard a nasty rumour that you're not staying for long. Tell me it's not true.'

'I'm sorry, my love. I have to go.'

'When?'

'Tonight.'

'That's what I'd heard, but I'd told myself I wasn't going to believe it until I'd heard it from you directly.'

'If I had any choice...'

'If any of us had any choice...'

'If I could—'

'—then I know you'd stay. Are things really as bad as they're saying, Robert?'

He turned away, not wanting her to see the hopelessness in his eyes. 'Worse,' he admitted.

'We're hearing all kinds of things, my love. Fantastic things. *Horrific* things.'

'All true. In fact, I'll wager you haven't heard the half of it. And that's why I have to go back.'

'But why you? There are plenty of other men.'

'Regrettably not. It seems I've acquired some kind of expertise in the colonel's eyes. There really is no choice.'

'It's so damn unfair.'

'I know, Jocelyn, but...'

'What?'

'But I fear if I don't do this, I might not have a home to come back to before long. There's an evil army fighting its way through mainland Europe, borne of the Third Reich, but having no place on Earth.'

'I want to ask you more, but I fear I wouldn't want to hear what you would tell me.'

'This is a foe which has an immeasurable advantage on the battlefield, an enemy which adds to its number with every fresh kill. And it's not just soldiers... ordinary people caught up in battle through sheer bad luck and geography... the innocents who...'

He stopped speaking. Tears were running freely down Jocelyn's cheeks.

'Stop, Robert... please. No more. I can't bear the thought of you going back into battle against these creatures. I'm terrified that next time you won't return.'

'Nothing and no one will stop me getting back to you, Jocelyn. It's the thought of us being together which will keep me alive and keep me fighting. I'll come home, my love, I promise.'

THE BRIEFING ROOM
21:00 HRS

The plan sounded simple. But then again, thought Wilkins, they usually did. Sitting here in the comfort and relative safety of the manor house, studying blurred photographs and hand-drawn maps, listening to intelligence reports and weather forecasts, the task at hand sounded decidedly less daunting than it should have.

The men gathered in the room were a mix of Brits and Yanks. Wilkins looked around, feeling like the odd one out as they all seemed to know each other. This mission had evidently been in planning for some time, just awaiting confirmation that the scientist was still at Polonezköy and additional intelligence from himself and others. The Yanks were from the 84th Airborne, and had been here at the manor house for the best part of a week, undergoing training alongside a small British task force. Captain Hunter was the American lead. He'd an accent so thick it had taken Wilkins a while to acclimatise to it. Even now he frequently misheard words. Not such a big deal had they just been enjoying a conversation in the pub on a Saturday afternoon, but to misconstrue an order in combat could be fatal. The stakes were far higher where they were going.

Colonel Adams ran through specifics of the mission, using a long stick to point out salient information on a blackboard mounted on the wall at the far end of the room. The colonel banged and scraped the stick, and the noise cut right through Wilkins. Was it just nerves, he wondered? He didn't feel himself at all. If he could have left the room without retribution and never returned, he thought he probably would. He did what he could to remain focused, but couldn't help remembering that buried deep below where he was sitting was one of the undead. It was frightening to think that one drop of blood, one splash of spittle, one bite, one scratch, one dribble of mucus, might be enough to unleash the unstoppable contagion on his beloved homeland.

Captain Hunter's men would provide cover to enable the Brits to gain access to the camp, find the scientist and extract him alive. His name was Doctor Egil Månsson, and they had been provided with the most recent photograph available. They all knew full well that being held in a concentration camp would inevitably have had dramatic effects on the doctor's appearance. At best he'd no doubt be weak and malnourished. There was every chance he wouldn't even be alive.

The task force was to be led by Lieutenant Charlie Henshaw, who had already wasted no time in letting Wilkins know who was in charge. Wilkins knew of Henshaw by reputation. Respected and loathed in equal measure, he got the job done and that was all that mattered tonight.

Sergeant Boris Steele was Henshaw's number two. He struck Wilkins as a decent chap, willing to listen and take a step back when he needed to, but equally prepared to stand his ground. He seemed to offer a welcome counterpoint to Lieutenant Henshaw's abrasiveness. There was no mistaking the high regard in which Steele held his closest comrades. Somewhat older than most of the men, he had a fatherly air about him.

Lance Corporals Harris, Barton and Jones were also along for the ride, and though Wilkins didn't know any of them, they all seemed like decent fellows. Wilkins thought that Jones, an enthusiastic scouser, didn't look old enough to be out alone this late, let alone to be parachuting deep into enemy territory. He was a diminutive lad who seemed to have trouble filling his own uniform.

'The main thing you need to know about Polonezköy right now is that it's been awful quiet over the last week or so,' a bespectacled intelligence officer explained.

'They stopped using it?' one of the Americans asked. 'Shut it down?'

'We're not sure. All we know is that movement around the camp has reduced to practically nothing.'

'Think they've cleared out?' another man asked.

The intelligence officer clearly had little in the way of useful intelligence to offer. 'I'm afraid we don't know. Even if the Germans have left the camp, there's been no major activity. That would indicate the prisoner population is still being held there.'

'Left to rot,' the first American seethed. 'That'd be right. Damn krauts.'

Colonel Adams took over and explained that the plan was to be dropped in a barren region a couple of miles south-west of Polonezköy. Captain Hunter's men would hold position long enough to ensure the task force had reached the camp, then move several miles north to take – and hold – the airfield at Leginów. There they'd wait for the Brits to return with their precious cargo, then call in air support so they could get out and get home.

Perhaps Wilkins wouldn't have felt like such an outsider if he'd been the first choice for the mission. But, as Colonel Adams had pointed out on more than one occasion with his customary lack of tact, the first choice officer was dead. As was the second choice. And the third. And the fourth was missing in action.

Shortly it was Wilkins' turn to step up to the front of the room to brief those who hadn't yet had the misfortune of facing the dead directly. He felt he needed to make them understand the magnitude of the threat which they had been tasked with trying to contain. The information he imparted was met with a curious mix of concern and incredulity. He thought they'd all grasp the seriousness of the situation soon enough. Indeed, the direness of his warnings was compounded with an update from the front: the US troops to the north and south of the German advance continued to struggle to hold back the undead masses. At the western tip of the bulge, where the British 6th Airborne and 53rd Infantry Division fought to contain the Nazis, the first contact with the ungodly creatures had been reported east of Namur.

The briefing was all but complete, and yet Colonel Adams didn't dismiss the men. He had still more to say. He cleared his throat and looked around the room. 'Gentlemen, please hear me out. You are all of you under the most extreme pressure imaginable, and I am well aware that I am sending you into one of the most – if not *the* most – dangerous places on the face of the Earth today, but I fear I must increase that pressure still further. Understand this, your mission must succeed. There is no room for failure. The undead scourge simply cannot be allowed to continue its progress unchecked. I feel I have a duty to tell you all that there is an alternative solution should your mission be a failure.'

Absolute silence. Not a movement. Not a murmur.

'The Americans are developing a weapon of untold power. Whilst I do not have any specifics – and some of you yanks here in the room with us today might – I have it on good authority that this new bomb could change the direction of the war with a single blast. I hope to goodness that such an awful weapon is used sparingly in battle, but consider this: if we are unable to stop the progress of our new ungodly enemy, total annihilation of great swathes of mainland Europe may be our only alternative. This is no understatement. The weight of the entire world rests on your shoulders tonight, men. God speed to you, and God help us all.'

THE WESTERN FRONT NEAR NAMUR

The British had continued to hold back the German advance, even reverse it for a time, but the battle was taking its toll. Sergeant Daniel Phillips was losing track of the days. He seemed to have been stuck in this damned spot forever. He and his men had taken over a derelict farmhouse just east of Namur, and from there they'd beaten back the advancing enemy again and again and again. Each time the Germans seemed to just keep coming. Phillips had, for a while, wondered if they'd been fighting those unstoppable undead monsters he continued to hear so much about. It was reassuring to see that when he shot a man these days, he still stayed down.

'All right there, Sergeant?' Private Harry Wilson asked, nudging Phillips in the ribs.

'I'm all right, Wilson,' he answered quickly. Instinctively. Better to give an immediate and flippant answer like that than to get bogged down in reality. It was hard being out here like this, damn hard. They all felt it, and it wasn't getting any easier. 'Keep talking will you, there's a good chap.'

'But you're usually telling me to shut up, sir,' he said in his broad Yorkshire accent. His voice was deep and wide. It sounded too old for the soldier's youthful face.

'I know, but occasionally I like to hear you talk rubbish. It reminds me of home.'

'Hear a lot of rubbish at home did you, sir?'

'That's not the point I'm making and you know it. Your accent is irrefutably British.'

'As is yours, sir. Yours is a bit more proper than mine, that's all.'

'It's not about status, it's about geography,' Phillips told him. 'Now tell us some of your bloody awful jokes. It's Christmas, after all.'

'Very well, sir. Why did the penny stamp?'

'Because the thruppenny bit,' someone shouted from another corner of the ransacked farmhouse kitchen.

'Very good,' Wilson laughed. 'Right, try this one. What did the sea say to the shore?'

'Nothing, it just waved,' another voice offered from the other side of an open door.

'We've heard these all before,' a third man said.

'I came here to kill Germans, not tell jokes,' Wilson reminded them. 'You don't win wars by telling jokes.'

'And thank goodness for that,' Phillips said, chuckling to himself. 'With your jokes we wouldn't have a hope in hell!'

For the moment, the farmhouse was filled with noise and good cheer.

In war, everything can change in a heartbeat.

Phillips and his men were resting. Fred McCarthy was on lookout, watching from the hayloft of an adjacent barn. It had been quiet these last few hours, and Private Neville was due to relieve him in thirty minutes or so, so he allowed himself to lie back in the shadows and close his eyes for the briefest of moments. It was all clear outside, not a soul to be seen in any direction. He wasn't going to sleep, he just wanted to rest for a while and get out of the icy breeze which gusted through the open hatch.

Private McCarthy had chosen the worst possible moment to lower his guard. When Neville stepped out of the farmhouse to cross the short distance to the barn, he thought his eyes were deceiving him. They had to be. How could so many of them have got here so quickly and so quietly? Hundreds of men approaching, revealed by the moonlight.

But this was no illusion. The ungodly Nazi army had reached the western front.

'Attack! We're under attack!' McCarthy shouted, and he doubled-back to the farmhouse when he saw several of the figures up ahead break into awkward sprints and come hurtling towards him. By the time he'd made it indoors his comrades were crowding every available window, firing at the shadowy shapes which swarmed silently nearer.

Sergeant Phillips took up position and began firing. 'Hit them with everything we have,' he shouted to his men. The moonlight struck the frost and snow and made everything appear brighter than it should have at this early hour. Phillips took aim and fired at one man who'd chosen to move criminally slowly. He hit him square in his chest, knocked him off his feet. But then he picked himself up again and continued his unsteady advance.

Phillips knew exactly what this meant.

The undead.

There were hundreds here, and there would be thousands more marching behind them.

From his hayloft look-out, Private McCarthy could see untold numbers emerging from the forest.

There'd be no more sleep here tonight.

THE SKIES OVER POLAND
00:30 HRS

Several hours later, and hundreds of miles away, and Wilkins could still taste Jocelyn's last kiss on his lips.

They baled out south of Polonezköy as planned, the men dropping from a relatively low height in quick succession, their rapid descent camouflaged by two Hawker Typhoons which circled and dived in the air well away from the landing site, putting on a firework show to distract the enemy and divert their attention away from Polonezköy.

It was a low altitude drop where time played tricks on the mind, slowing down and speeding up at the same time. The ground – unremittingly dark here, disorientating – rushed towards Wilkins and the others. There was a huge amount to do to arrest and control their descent: checking body position, deploying the canopy, turning into the wind and preparing to land, and – most importantly – keeping a look-out. Lieutenant Henshaw scanned the area beneath his dangling feet, watching out for signs of enemy movement whilst planning where he was going to touch down and which way he'd run and lead his men. It was almost completely black and devoid of life. Nothing to be seen anywhere.

It was all over in seconds, barely enough time.

He looked up and saw the outline of the Douglas from which they'd just baled; a dark silhouette climbing away through the black-purple night. Beyond it one of the Typhoons, drawing distant enemy fire. And, just for a second, over the tops of the trees he saw the outline of Polonezköy camp. It was a severe, gothic-looking place, and it unnerved him more than the prospect of a difficult landing or engagement with enemy troops.

Focus.

No time left.

Lieutenant Henshaw hit the ground and immediately executed a textbook parachute landing fall, transferring the force of impact from his feet and ankles and rolling away. He was up again in a heartbeat, detaching himself from his chute and swiftly rolling up the nylon material, acutely aware how prone a target it made him to any watching eyes.

The others.

He looked around the vast field where he'd touched down. He could see Harris and Barton doing the same thing as him, both of them no more than fifty yards from his position. Sergeant Steele was touching down the same distance away again, whilst Jones still had a little distance left to descend. All around them, Americans came down like rain.

One missing. A single member of the British task force so far unaccounted for. He span around.

'Looking for me, Lieutenant?'

Wilkins was standing directly behind him, parachute already dealt with and safely stashed away. Henshaw wasn't yet sure what he thought about Wilkins. He was an unknown quantity. 'Let's go,' he said abruptly, avoiding conversation.

The tundra-like field in which they'd landed was empty, but it was also deceptively hard to navigate because of the layer of fine, powder-like snow which hid the unpredictable undulations of the frozen ground. A myriad of tracks and grooves had been worn into the mud and had frozen hard as concrete. Henshaw gestured for his men to follow the Americans' lead and head for the trees to the north. Although pitch-black at this late hour, the moon was high in the sky and it frequently peeked out from behind the clouds and filled the world with unwanted glimmers of light, picking out the definition the soldiers preferred to hide, illuminating the edges of everything.

The first of the dead came towards them with a flagrant disregard for its own safety. It had been a local man once, a farmer perhaps. Unarmed. 'Think this guy needs help?' a GI innocently asked. He was puzzled by the fact the man wore only casual clothing, no protection against the bitter cold.

Wilkins broke ranks and ran forward to intercept him, and dealt with him swiftly with his clasp knife before returning to the others. Several Americans looked at him in confusion, not having faced the undead on the battlefield previously. 'It's the only way,' he explained. 'No gunfire, you'll just draw them to us quicker. There are several villages nearby, all as quiet as the camp by all accounts. I'll wager they're all like this. I'll bet there's no one left alive here tonight.'

Captain Hunter nodded. 'You heard the lieutenant,' he said to his troops. 'Keep your eyes open for these things, and do what he just did if and when you have to. Now keep the noise to a minimum and move.'

The soldiers set off in the direction of the airfield. Captain Hunter dispatched scouts deeper into the forest, and the rest of the men moved as a pack. They encountered another couple of dead Poles, but they were dealt with quickly and easily.

'It's somewhat easier when you're on the move,' Wilkins said to the captain. 'The real concern is when you stop. They'll group around you, gravitate to your noise. Be careful when you reach the airfield, sir. They're capable of moving in herds like cattle.'

'Appreciate the advice, Lieutenant Wilkins, but my men and I have this covered.' Captain Hunter stopped and turned to face the rest of the Brits. 'We'll get you close to the outer fence, and you're on your own from there. We'll be waiting at the rendezvous point at dawn, understand?'

'Understood, Captain,' Lieutenant Henshaw replied. 'Your support and the support of your men is very much appreciated.'

'Show us your gratitude by being ready and being on time. First light and we're out of here. We'll be gone by eight, no later.'

'We'll be there.'

'Whether you're there or not isn't my concern, lieutenant. I'll say it again, *we'll be gone*. This place don't feel right to me. Too quiet...'

The captain returned his attention to his men, giving out more orders in hushed tones as they continued through the trees.

The six British men were grouped together. Wilkins was the odd man out, and his unease was clear. 'What's the matter with him?' Harris asked, his voice just loud enough for him to hear. Wilkins thought his cockney accent sounded unexpectedly abrasive and out of place here.

'There's nothing wrong with me, as it happens,' Wilkins said, decidedly unimpressed at being spoken about as if he wasn't there. 'You'd do well to keep your mouth shut and listen out.'

'What, for more dead men walking?'

Wilkins was angered by his mocking tone. 'You'll not be laughing when you're facing your first one.'

'All of us, fully armed, and you still think the dead'll be a match for us, Lieutenant? I saw the way you killed that last one.'

'One is easy to deal with, but these things can come in vast numbers.'

'We'll cross that particular bridge when we come to it.'

'Let's have this conversation again when we get home, Lance Corporal. *If* we get home. I'll remind you of your comments.'

'You do that, sir.'

'Cut it out,' Henshaw warned, already tired of the bickering. It was down to nerves, he was sure. He was prepared to give his men the benefit of the doubt. For now.

'Awful quiet here,' Lance Corporal Harris observed. 'I thought Fritz would have been all over this place.'

'It's a dead zone,' Lieutenant Henshaw explained. 'Isn't that right, Lieutenant Wilkins?'

'Yes, it is.'

'What, dead as in them dead things walking about?' Barton asked, nervously looking over his shoulder.

'No, dead as in completely empty,' Wilkins corrected him. 'Ever been to Australia, soldier?'

'I hadn't been out of Blighty until a few months back,' Barton replied. 'Why?'

'Because they have an enormous problem with bushfires in Australia, and this is how they try and keep the problem under control.'

'You've completely lost me now.'

'They call it a fire-break. They get ahead of the fire and burn away a strip of land, sometimes more than a mile wide. Then when the bushfire reaches the strip that's already been burned, there's no fuel left to keep the flames burning and it extinguishes itself.'

'I still don't follow...'

'Come on, Barton, don't be such a dolt,' Henshaw sighed. 'He can't make it any plainer. We've a problem with the undead attacking other folks and adding to their number, so what's the best way of stopping them doing that right now?'

Barton shrugged his shoulders.

'Get rid of their prey,' Harris answered on behalf of his slow-to-catch-on colleague. 'Crikey, Barton, you ain't the brightest spark.'

'Gentlemen,' Henshaw warned, 'this is neither the time nor the place for bickering. Let us stay focused on the task at hand, shall we.'

Sufficiently rebuffed, the men became quiet and continued to move forward.

'First people ever to try and break into a bloody Nazi concentration camp...' Harris mumbled to himself.

The border of Polonezköy reared up out of the forest, ominous and apparently impenetrable. A tall electrified outer fence and an equally tall wall beyond. The Brits had pored over low-quality aerial photographs and best-guess schematics before leaving Pocklington Hall, trying to piece together the ground plans to this unspeakably horrific place. The boundary of the camp, still a distance beyond the trees, appeared featureless and unending from here, as if there was nothing beyond it, literally the end of the world.

Captain Hunter called over to Lieutenant Henshaw. 'This is where we split. You're on your own from here. See you at the rendezvous in about seven hours.'

Before Henshaw could reply, the captain and his men were gone. Henshaw gathered the rest of his crew around. 'We're going in from the rear of the camp. We need to dig under the electrified fence, then find the best spot to try and get over the wall.'

He had been wondering how operational the camp would still be. After all, the intelligence reports they'd heard back at base had indicated that very little, if any activity had been observed here. Lance Corporal Barton, a quiet, reflective man at the best of times, had barely spoken since they'd touched down in Poland. He too had been considering the condition of the camp. 'So what do you reckon, lieutenant? Are they all dead in there? Is this going to be easier than we thought?'

'Nothing's easy in war, you know that.'

'And dead doesn't mean dead anymore, either,' Wilkins added ominously.

'Fact is, we don't know what we'll find until we're inside. What we do know is that this is the place where the Nazis created and tested their serum, so there's a strong possibility that many of the current occupants of Polonezköy might already have acceded to the undead condition. I'll wager the place has been tightly locked down to prevent the germ from spreading.'

'Remember what I said about the fire-break?' Wilkins added. 'We have to remember, the effects of the serum do not respect side, rank, or any other difference. It's highly likely that if the infection has run wild in there, the entire populations of both prisoners and guards of the camp will be infected now.'

'I've got to admit,' Barton said, 'despite what we heard in the briefing, I still expected searchlights and sirens and all the usual bells and whistles.'

'The silence is somehow more concerning, isn't it?'

'So if they're all dead—' Sergeant Steele said.

'Or undead,' Jones muttered.

'—then what about this scientist chap we're here for?'

'Yes, he may already be dead too,' Henshaw admitted. 'But we still need to find him. One way or another, we have to locate Egil Månsson.'

'And if he's one of *them*?' Jones asked. 'They said the best way to deal with them was to damage their brains. How's this scientist gonna be any good to anyone if his brain don't work?'

'Well you seem to manage all right, Jones,' Henshaw said, rapidly losing patience. 'Right, we're wasting time. Let's move.'

A crackle of noise. Blue static flashes. Flames.

The men held their collective breath and watched the fence around Polonezköy intently. Something had just collided with the electrified wire-mesh and proved beyond doubt that, in spite of the ominous darkness everywhere, the power was still running. Henshaw used his binoculars to try and see what it was that had hit the fence. 'What is it, sir?' asked Harris. Henshaw didn't answer, he just passed his field-glasses across.

Harris found it hard to comprehend what he was seeing. It was a Nazi guard, already almost completely consumed by flames, and he was gripping the fence tight, oblivious to the agonising pain he should have been feeling. Harris watched in disbelief as the soldier simply let go and walked away, managing to make it another twenty yards or so before the flames overtook him and he dropped to the ground, muscle and sinew burned away to nothing.

OUTSIDE POLONEZKÖY

Jones and Steele knew exactly what to do. They emerged from the shadowed tree-line and ran towards the fence around the concentration camp, keeping low despite being quite certain that no one was watching. The barbed-wire topped mesh fence seemed to tower above them – far too high and dangerous to scale even if it hadn't been electrified. They chose a spot which was easy to remember: just to the right of another enormous elm tree and, according to the lieutenant's map, at a point near a part of the camp complex which was relatively infrequently accessed.

Both men took entrenching tools from their packs and began to dig, working at pace and managing to quickly excavate a decent amount of soil, no mean feat given that much of it was hard as concrete, rock-solid with permafrost. It wasn't going to be easy to dig under the fence, but it appeared to be their only option tonight. The constant electric hum of the barrier was enough to ensure that both men constantly kept their wits about them.

Henshaw dispatched Harris to try and get a better appreciation of what was happening inside the camp. He slipped back into the trees and soon found an oak which appeared tall enough and strong enough and which was relatively easy to climb. The branches, although bare, would provide enough cover in the low light. He shimmied up the trunk and found himself a good spot.

Even in almost total darkness, Polonezköy camp was a terrifying sight. It had been built in the grounds of a castle which dated back to the sixteenth century, with the imposing gothic entrance of the castle itself acting as the single entry and exit point. Harris' stomach churned with nerves, and he could only begin to imagine what the prisoners, already broken and resigned to their fate, must have felt when they arrived at the camp to be greeted with such an imposing façade.

The vast area enclosed by the border fence and the wall just beyond was difficult to make out from up here. He could just about make out the roofs of low huts and other buildings, grey against the gloom, and a couple of guard towers which appeared to be unmanned. There were occasional glowing lights in places, but nothing like the level of illumination he'd expected to see there. Harris was a tough soldier who'd faced more than his fair share of unspeakable horrors during his relatively short years of service, but there was something about Polonezköy this morning that unsettled him more than anything he'd come across before today. It seemed to have a brooding menace all of its own. He knew the camp was packed full of people. Whether they were alive or not was a different question (and he was pretty sure it was a question to which he already knew the answer). It was like they were waiting for the task force to try and break in. Like they were lurking in the shadows, ready to jump out. Thousands of them.

Harris held his position and kept a close watch until they were ready to make their move.

Jones and Steele worked hard and fast with their entrenching tools, moving with unspoken synchronicity as they took turns to dig in and shift more frozen soil, all the time taking care not to touch the electrified fence. The sergeant led by example, easily matching the younger man's pace.

The smell of burnt flesh still hung heavy in the air from the thing that had made contact with the deadly barrier a short time earlier, a stark reminder of the dangers they faced. Henshaw, Wilkins and Barton watched from the near distance until the two men began to visibly flag. 'Barton, we'll take over for a stretch,' Henshaw said.

Wilkins was keen to gain the trust and respect of the others. 'You stay here, Lieutenant, and I'll go. I don't want to be accused of shirking. You've got your men to look after.'

'Very good. Thank you, Wilkins.'

He and Barton swapped places with the pair at the fence. Wilkins was impressed by the amount of work which had already been done: the hole was wide enough and deep enough to crawl into, just not yet quite long enough to reach over to the other side of the electrified fence. It soon would be, though. He worked hard to match Barton's pace, but made a mental note to try and conserve his energy. Despite the physical effort breaking in was taking, he knew the real work would begin once they were on the inside, and there would be no time to catch their breath once the camp wall had been breached. He had in his mind that the next few hours would be something of a sprint; a war conducted at breakneck speed.

Twenty minutes more and they were just about through. Near the trees, Harris returned to report back to Lieutenant Henshaw. 'It's really not right in there, Lieutenant.'

'What's that supposed to mean?'

'Dunno, sir. Can't rightly put my finger on it. Most of the lights are out, and I couldn't see any movement from where I was. I think it's every bit as bad as Lieutenant Wilkins reckons.'

'We have to be positive. Fewer lights and fewer guards might mean it's easier for us once we're inside.'

'Here's hoping, sir,' Harris said, praying the low moonlight was dull enough to disguise his unease.

Barton jogged back over. 'We're through, Lieutenant.'

Henshaw nodded at Jones. 'Right. You're up next, Lance Corporal. You know what to do.'

With trepidation wrote clear on his mud and sweat-stained face, Jones stripped down to his vest and walked towards the fence, teeth chattering with cold. The others took his gear. 'We call him the rat,' Barton explained to Wilkins. 'And not just because of his looks, neither. He's a slippery little bugger. Can just about get through any gap we need him to.'

And he was right. The hole they'd dug under the fence was relatively shallow, but it was deep enough for Jones who half-crawled, half-dragged himself through, seeming to contort his torso to a remarkable degree to avoid touching the wire. 'He could have been in the circus,' Harris laughed.

'A deserter from the big top,' Steele agreed.

'All right, all right... that's enough,' Henshaw snapped. 'We need to focus. There'll be time for laughs when we're safely back in Blighty.'

Jones looked up as the others neared. He was on the other side of the fence now with the entrenching tool he'd pushed ahead of him, working hard to increase the size of the hole so his colleagues and all their kit could fit through. He didn't like being over on this side on his own. His teeth were chattering with nerves now as much as cold, and his guts were tied up in knots.

APPROACHING THE AIRFIELD AT LEGINÓW

Captain Hunter and his men reached the airfield with only minor inconvenience from a handful of rogue corpses. Some of the soldiers appeared overly keen to try their hand at 're-killing' (as someone had named it) and almost fought with each other to be among the first ones to attack. Hunter let them have their moment. He'd felt all along that there'd be plenty of opportunities to face this new unnatural foe.

And he was soon proved right.

The airfield at Leginów appeared barely equipped to support any kind of military activity. It was little more than a long, roughly rectangular field with a number of small, hut-like buildings at the far end. A camouflaged hangar stood off to the right.

Hunter split his men, one group advancing along each side of the makeshift runway which, had it not been for the tell-tale grooves left in the frozen mud and long patchy strips of flattened grass, would have been indistinguishable from any other field in any other place. There was some movement in the trees nearby, but the soldiers were able to advance with such well-practiced stealth that they passed by the dead unnoticed.

The groups converged near the hangar. Hunter sent a couple of his best men inside, Sergeants Hennessy and O'Rourke. They were in and out in a couple of minutes and wasted no time reporting back. 'Looks clear, Captain,' Hennessy said. 'I mean it's empty and all, but no surprises.'

'Good, good. Looks like we got the better end of the deal then, eh boys. We get to protect an airfield that don't much need protecting.'

'Can we get inside, sir?' a kid called Rumbelow asked. The adrenalin had worn off, and cold was setting in.

'Don't see why not. Mudriczki and Carter, take a couple more fellas and get those huts checked out. The rest of you, let's get in out of the cold.'

Jimmy Mudriczki led the men over to the first of the huts. He peered inside through an ice-covered window but could see little. Definitely no movement. Nat Carter looked in from the opposite side. 'Looks okay, Jimmy,' he said.

'Yeah, this place is like the grave. No one here. Anyone with any sense is long gone. Get the door and let's get this done.'

The two other men – Coles and Willard – took up position just to the rear of Carter as he leaned across and pushed the door open.

The hut was booby-trapped.

The building exploded, billowing flames and searing heat filling the night air. The noise echoed like a gunshot. Mudriczki, Carter and Coles were killed instantly. Willard staggered away from the wreck, his smock on fire, trying to put himself out. Other men were there in seconds to help, but they all knew it was too little, too late.

The trap had had the desired effect. A horrific parting shot from the krauts who'd fled Polonezköy.

All around, the dead turned towards the airfield and began their lethargic advance.

Hundreds of them.

INSIDE POLONEZKÖY

Within the hour the Brits had all made it across the wire. They leaned against the wall which stood between them and Polonezköy's inmates. They were making plans to go over the top when Barton grabbed hold of Harris. 'Guard approaching,' he hissed, and the message was quickly passed from man to man. They each pressed themselves against the wall, hidden in the low light and shadow, and watched as the lone figure neared. The Nazi officer was moving lethargically and aimlessly; not so much patrolling, more like staggering...

Nervous glances were exchanged. Barton reached for his pistol but Wilkins stopped him and took his knife from the pocket of his Denison smock. He held a finger to his lips.

The enemy officer lurched closer, and though the limited illumination made it hard to discern any great level of detail, they saw enough to know that he was in a wretched condition. His face was covered in blood, one eye bulging from its socket as if it was trying to escape. 'He one of them?' Jones whispered to Lieutenant Wilkins.

'Almost certainly,' Wilkins whispered back as he readied himself to strike. But Sergeant Steele had other ideas.

'This bastard's mine,' he announced, and he stepped out in front of the Nazi. He grabbed Jerry's head in a tight neck lock.

'Watch his bite...' Wilkins warned, but Steele wasn't listening, nor was he concerned. He took a fistful of the German's hair and pulled his head back, then drew his own blade across his throat. A large, dark gash appeared in the dead man's pale flesh, curved like a lecherous grin, and thick, dark semi-coagulated blood flowed like glistening mud down the front of his grubby-looking uniform tunic.

Steele pushed the Nazi away. Job done.

Yet Jerry didn't stop.

His head lolled awkwardly, and the glutinous blood continued to seep, but his progress and intent appeared otherwise unimpeded until Wilkins took control. He shoved the Nazi's face against the wall, then stabbed his knife into the man's exposed right temple. He withdrew the blade then did it again, then a third time to be sure, then he let him go. Jerry immediately collapsed like a half-stuffed rag doll. Henshaw shone a torch into his face, checking for any reaction. The flow of blood had partially obscured the Totenkopf symbol patch on the guard's right collar. It was clear that this man had been a member of the SS-Totenkopfverbände. 'Good Lord,' he exclaimed. 'If evil bastards like this have been overcome by this hideous disease, what hope is there for any of us?'

'So I take it that you believe everything you've heard now, gentlemen?' Wilkins asked. 'This is no joke, no trick... These creatures are the reanimated bodies of the dead, and I'll wager there are many, many more of the damn things waiting for us on the other side of this wall. We need to have our wits about us. We must treat everyone and everything we see in there as a potential threat, do you understand?'

He didn't need to hear their replies to know that they did.

The soldiers moved quickly and quietly to scale the wall. Henshaw had deliberately chosen this spot as he considered it to be the part of the camp under the least amount of scrutiny and guard from the Nazis. This was the area where they disposed of bodies. And here there were many, many bodies to dispose of.

Henshaw ordered Harris to use a grappling hook to scale the wall. The clattering of metal on brick was unnaturally loud against the all-consuming quiet of everything else. The soldiers stood silently with their backs against the wall for several minutes until they were sure the noise hadn't attracted more unwanted attention. Harris climbed up and paused at the top to look down over the other side. 'Courtyard's empty,' he hissed to the others. 'Should be all right, sir.'

'Good. Drop down and keep out of sight.'

He did as he was ordered and the rest of the men followed in quick succession. Steele was the last one. Perched precariously on the top of the wall until he was sure the others were down safely, he detached the grappling hook and spooled the rope, then dropped it down to Harris who stashed it in Barton's pack.

Behind the imposing castle entrance and within the vast encircling wall of the camp were several clearly defined areas. Nearest the castle were the barracks of the SS-Totenkopfverbände. Next to the barracks, a half-full vehicle compound. Beyond that, more than half the total area of the site was occupied by large factory buildings where the prisoners were put to work by the Nazis. Most of the smaller, squat, dank-looking huts were almost certainly where the prisoners were housed, separated into sub-areas: one for men, the other for women and children. The part of the camp where they'd gained access, though, was unspeakably grim. Wilkins was glad of the lack of light. There were things here he had no desire to see. Jones, on the other hand, exhibited far less self-control. 'Bloody hell,' he cursed, forgetting himself. 'Look at all this...'

He shone a torch in a wide circle over a space to the rear of where they were standing. They knew the Nazi's preferred methods of extermination from the intelligence which had been gathered, but what they could see now was way beyond anything they'd been told.

'Crikey,' Barton mumbled, barely able to string two words together. 'It's like they ran out of space and time.'

He was right. His description was remarkably apt and succinct. Many of the bodies appeared to have been carved up, limbs dismembered and stacked in hotchpotch piles. Jones was transfixed by the horrific sight, and it took his sergeant's firm grip to drag him away. 'Come on, lad,' Steele said. 'Focus.'

Jones tried, but it was difficult. Before turning away he looked again at a particular mound of flesh which had been momentarily illuminated by his torch. He was sure he'd seen fingers moving on a hand sticking out from the bottom of a pile. And he could see the remains of Nazi uniforms too. He wondered what had really happened in Polonezköy, and wished with all his heart that he was anywhere but here.

Focus!

Another figure was moving across the courtyard now, coming towards the British soldiers with the same uneasy slothfulness as the German guard they'd already dispatched. Wait... more than one. Wilkins counted three of them. It was clear that their overall physical condition was very different to the undead Nazi. 'Good Lord,' said Henshaw, 'they're prisoners. What in heaven's name are they doing out here like this? They'll get themselves killed.'

But they were already dead.

The three men approaching were each dressed in the same loose-fitting, shapeless uniforms, and whilst the colour might originally have been relatively standard, it was now anything but. Harris shone a flashlight at them, and the sorry state of these poor lost souls was clearly revealed. Their smocks were stained and smeared, deep red and brown patches where blood and other discharge had seeped from open wounds which would now never heal.

'What do we do, Lieutenant?' Harris asked, clearly unsure. Henshaw glanced at Wilkins before answering.

'We get rid of them. We don't have any choice.'

'But they're innocent men...' Steele started to protest. Wilkins cut across him.

'They're dead, Sergeant, and you need to remember that. Ending this eternal misery is the kindest thing we can do for them now.'

Wilkins stepped forward with his knife again and went for the nearest of the three. The man's awkward gait and poorly controlled movements resulted in him virtually stepping onto Wilkins' blade and skewering himself. Wilkins quickly yanked the knife clear then went for the dead man's head. He pushed the suddenly lifeless figure out of the way and was ready to move onto the next but Jones was there first.

'Don't!' Wilkins exclaimed, but it was too late. Jones shot both of the other prisoners in the head in quick succession.

The noise echoed around the emptiness of the concentration camp, seeming to take forever to completely fade away.

'What the hell were you thinking, Jones?' demanded Henshaw.

'Dealing with the situation, sir.'

'And did you not listen to anything Lieutenant Wilkins had to say about the threat we're facing?'

Wilkins himself was furious. 'Good grief, man. Do you realise what you've done?'

Jones shone his torch from side to side, and the true extent of the situation he'd created quickly became clear. All around them there was movement now. The shadows seemed to be detaching themselves from the walls. Unfolding. Unfurling. Untangling themselves from the darkness and creeping towards the light. And the longer the men looked, the more of them they could see, as if scores of the infernal creatures had been woken by Jones' two shots. The way they moved made their appearance all the more terrifying. They lurched and listed, contorted and twisted as if they were barely in control of their own physical form.

The nearest of them reached out for Jones and grabbed his smock with gnarled fingers, snagging the drab material. He hadn't realised and tried to back away, but was pulled back. Henshaw saw that one of his men was in trouble and instinctively moved to help him. Although he managed to prise the wretched ghoul away from Jones, all he did was drag the creature closer to himself, and when another one of them came at him he lost his footing in the gloom and was down before anyone realised.

'Blades, not bullets,' Wilkins hissed, and this time the other soldiers did as he instructed, fishing knives, daggers and even entrenching tools from their kit. Wilkins himself waded into the melee, and the others followed his lead.

Two more were disposed of by Wilkins in quick succession. He took the first one out through his tried and tested method of a sudden stab to the temple, then rammed its decaying face hard against the side of the nearest hut. He turned to take out the next one, but was immediately filled with uncomfortable, conflicting emotions because this figure had clearly once been a young woman. For a split second he felt overwhelming guilt, then remorse, then desperate fear when he realised this poor wretch couldn't have been very different in age when she'd died to his love, Jocelyn.

No room for emotions now. Everything depended on what happened here tonight. The pressure was immense. Almost unbearable.

It was impossible to be sure how many of the unspeakable fiends were converging on them now. Between them, Harris and Steele dispatched several more, the efficiency of their kills increasing with each one. Contrary to how the papers and the movies often portrayed it, there was nothing easy or glamorous about killing anyone in battle. In films you didn't have to deal with the blood or the stench or the cries for help or mercy. Films made killing look easy, effortless. Steele had just about become used to the guilt-tinged adrenalin rush he felt whenever he faced the Hun, but this was a different matter altogether. And as he struggled to deal with an emaciated prisoner's remains which fought with the tenacity of a trained SS Obersturmführer, he knew this was an even more terrifying enemy they were now having to face.

All of the doubts and misgivings these British soldiers might have had, the unspoken suspicions that Wilkins was wrong or that he'd exaggerated the situation in Europe, were all undone in the space of several frantic minutes.

A gap in the oncoming crowd. They must have faced twenty or thirty between them now, though numbers were unclear in the dark. Wilkins dashed across to Harris and Jones to help put down two more frenzied attackers. 'We need to get under cover,' he gasped breathlessly. 'Otherwise we'll be fighting like this all night. That's if we last that long. We've no idea how many of them there are.'

'The huts,' Steele shouted over the chaos, gesticulating wildly once he'd twisted the neck of a dead SS guard and put a blade through his eye.

'But we don't know what's in there, Sarge,' Jones said.

'No, but we *do* know what's out here,' Wilkins immediately replied.

He ran towards the nearest of the shabby wooden buildings, shoulder charging more of the dead out of the way now rather than wasting time and effort trying to deal with them more comprehensively. The others followed as best they could, kicking and lashing out at the hellish creatures which swarmed around them in huge numbers, apparently without end.

Wilkins yanked at the door. The handle was stiff but, to his surprise, opened relatively easily. Jones piled inside after him, followed by Steele. 'Where's Barton?' asked the sergeant, realising he was the last one who'd made it to cover, immediately concerned for the men. 'And Harris and the lieutenant? Where the hell are they?'

He had a Sten gun slung across his back. He swung it around and held it ready.

'Think about the bloody noise, man,' Wilkins said, doing his best to dissuade him from firing. He knew his words would inevitably have little effect.

'Bit late for that now, Lieutenant,' Steele said, and he kicked the door open again and charged back outside. Wilkins tried to stop him, but he was already running headlong into the still advancing crowd, firing wildly and filling the air with noise. It was clear that he was trying to create a distraction so that his colleagues would stand a chance of surviving. And it seemed to be working too, because those members of the army of the dead that Wilkins could see – prisoners and Nazis alike – were staggering further away from the hut now and following Steele into the impenetrable darkness elsewhere.

'Help me!'

The remaining Brits heard Harris' distinctive voice calling. Jones illuminated him with his torch and saw he was standing over the injured Lieutenant Henshaw, doing everything he could to keep great swathes of venomous corpses at bay. He was swinging a shovel he'd happened upon from somewhere. The head of the spade made contact with the skull of one of the dead, filling the air with a sonorous clang and sending the pitiful creature spiralling away.

Wilkins punched his blade hard into the face of one of the undead. He moved forward, but was then forced to rock back on his toes to avoid being caught with the edge of the scything shovel blade. 'Steady on, Harris,' he exclaimed. 'It's me, Wilkins.'

No time for pleasantries. 'Help the lieutenant,' Harris yelled. 'Get him under cover. He's hurt.'

Barton appeared from nowhere and helped Wilkins pick the fallen officer up off the ground. The two of them half-carried, half-dragged him back to the hut. Harris followed, still wildly swinging the shovel as he backed towards the others, cutting down more relentless bodies with every vicious swipe. The moment they were all inside Barton snatched the shovel from him and used it to wedge the door shut.

'That should hold the buggers back for a while,' he said. He could see shapeless figures crowding on the other side of the windows. He couldn't make out any level of detail, but just knowing they were there was terrifying enough.

'What about the sarge?' Jones asked. He could still hear the Sten gun being fired repeatedly in the distance.

'Sergeant Steele will find his way back here soon enough,' Barton said. 'I hope,' he added under his breath.

The group's full attention shifted to the wounded officer writhing in pain at their feet. Wilkins crouched down next to him, checking his wounds. Henshaw's right arm was badly broken, that much was clear, and in the little he could see from the limited light of Jones' torch, his skin had already developed an unhealthy pallor.

'What do we do?' Jones asked. He sounded panicked, like a child.

'The first thing we do, Lance Corporal, is shut up,' Wilkins told him in no uncertain terms. 'Now get some more light down here, and someone find something I can use as a splint.'

Barton happened across a length of wooden baton. He propped it against the wall and snapped it in half with three hard stomps of his boot. Harris found two Feuerhand Hurricane lamps which he managed to get lit reasonably quickly, filling the hut with light.

'Where's the blood coming from?' asked Harris, and he moved closer with one of the lanterns. Blood was pooling behind the officer's back, spilling out across the wooden floor like a slick.

'I've no idea,' said Wilkins, and he carefully rolled Henshaw towards him to look at his back. Henshaw's smock and other clothing had been torn: slashed during the frenzied attack. With his heart in his mouth and fearing the worst, Wilkins lifted away several layers of blood-soaked material until Henshaw's bare skin was exposed. He looked like he'd been clawed by a bear.

'And here, sir,' Jones said, gingerly rolling up his commanding officer's crimson stained trouser leg. 'Look.'

In the glare of the kerosene lamp, Wilkins saw an unmistakable semi-circular mark. He'd been bitten. He stepped back from the fallen officer with a heavy heart. 'He's not going to make it,' he said.

'It's just a broken bone and a few scratches,' Jones protested. 'He'll be all right. We'll leave him here and—'

'You don't understand, Jones, he's infected. It's too much of a risk to leave him here like this. We have to deal with him in the same way we deal with those hideous things out there.'

'He's not dead.'

'He's as good as.'

Wilkins held his clasp knife ready, but Harris blocked the way. 'Lay one finger on Lieutenant Henshaw and you'll have me to answer to.'

'Listen to me, if the lieutenant dies, he'll come back. And your uniforms and allegiances and past histories will count for nothing. He'll attack and—'

'No, with all due respect, sir, you listen to me,' Harris interrupted. 'The lieutenant has seen me safely through many a scrape. I'm not going to turn my back on him now when he needs me most.'

Wilkins was ready to protest, but he knew it would do no good. He understood completely, but that didn't make the situation any easier to deal with. He reluctantly stepped away from Henshaw, but kept his clasp knife gripped tight in his hand.

The group's hasty entrance and subsequent bickering had aroused plenty of attention from the undead hordes outside, and whilst Steele had been able to draw many of them away, there were still a considerable number gathered around the front of the hut. 'We're blocked in,' Barton whispered. He'd been looking out through a small window. 'There's loads of them out there. We either fight our way out, or we wait.'

'We can't wait,' Wilkins reminded him. 'There's no time. If we're not at the rendezvous point by dawn, I fear we'll be spending the rest of our days here in Polonezköy.'

'Here,' Jones hissed from the other side of the shack. 'There's another door.'

He hesitated before opening it, fearing what he might find on the other side and picturing swarms more reanimated guards and prisoners emerging from the shadows and rushing towards him.

It was empty.

The connecting room was much larger than the first, and it was almost completely bare. Its purpose was immediately apparent. The stench of death hung heavy in the air, even stronger here than in the rest of this damned place. The remaining men left Henshaw and followed Jones inside. It was easy for each of them to stand here and picture it packed to the rafters with confused and frightened prisoners of war, brought to Polonezköy to be exterminated in their thousands.

With Henshaw wounded, Wilkins assumed command. He knew this would be a test of his diplomatic as well as his military skills. He stood with the others in the ante-room and cleared his throat to speak. 'Let's not forget why we are here, gentlemen. This camp, and other camps like it, are places of unspeakable horror where despicable acts are carried out with alarming regularity. The Nazis who operated this facility have shown no mercy to these innocent people, and now we shall show no mercy to them. If, in the hours ahead, you ever have cause to doubt what we are doing and why we are doing it, remember this room. Remember the awful feeling in your gut which I know you all have right now, just as I do. Remember the sense of dread that sits in your belly like vomit because you know you are in the presence of true evil.'

'Well said, sir,' Barton mumbled.

'Keep your heads, men, and remember what's at stake. We'd already been told that Polonezköy had fallen largely silent, and now we know why. What we have here is a microcosm – a scaled-down version of what will inevitably happen to the entire world if we don't do the job we've been sent here to do. Do you all understand?'

Even though their collective responses were low and subdued, it was clear that they did.

'So what's the plan?' Jones asked.

'Given the importance to the Reich of what was developed here, I'm convinced that Doctor Månsson's laboratory must be somewhere in the castle. Given the lack of human resistance we've encountered since arriving here, I suspect the Doctor himself has either been incarcerated or abandoned or both. I don't know what we'll find in there, but the castle and its keep is where we need to start our search. Once we have the doctor or, failing that, his research, we simply have to get out of this hellish place and make our way to the rendezvous site.'

'You make it sound so simple,' Barton said, barely managing to contain his sarcasm. Wilkins was not impressed.

'Mr Barton, I am under absolutely no illusions, and nor should you be. I knew this mission would be nigh on impossible from the outset, and nothing I've seen so far has convinced me otherwise. However, as we all know, the importance of what we're doing here cannot be overstated. Without us, the entire civilised world is as good as lost forever. The dead will inherit the Earth. Our families, friends and other loved ones will be slaughtered by the dead and will almost inevitably join their ranks. And if we are unsuccessful, we too face the same foul fate. We simply cannot afford to fail. The success of the mission must come first, no matter what the cost.'

As Wilkins spoke and the others listened, transfixed and terrified in equal measure, Lieutenant Henshaw gave out his last breath and died. Lying on the floor in the adjacent room, he became completely still.

'I suggest we find an alternative way out of this building,' Wilkins continued. 'If we're clever about this, we might be able to get out without those damn buggers on the other side of the door knowing what we're up to. With any luck they'll remain focused on this building in the belief that we're still inside.'

'Do we have any idea about the layout of the castle?' Harris asked.

'Barely anything,' Barton said.

'What's where don't matter,' Jones added. 'We just keep searching 'til we find what we want.'

'Exactly,' Wilkins said. 'We just need to—'

He was silenced by a godawful clattering from the room next door. It had been less than a minute, but the deadly germ already coursing through the late Lieutenant Henshaw's bloodstream had already caused him to reanimate. In his infected stupor he'd tried to support himself on his badly broken arm and had fallen heavily against a wall, riling the corpses outside still further.

Harris lifted his lamp and illuminated the deceased officer's death mask. It was a terrifying sight; so completely unnatural. So familiar, yet so unfamiliar at the same time. Dead Henshaw picked himself up again and staggered towards the light, his mouth hanging open, ready to bite and spread the deadly infection he carried. Harris froze.

Wilkins grabbed Henshaw by the scruff of the neck and spun him around, pushing him back against the wall. Yet more excitement rippled through the ranks of the foul crowd amassed outside at the noise. He raised his knife and did what he had to do. Henshaw twitched and jerked for a moment on the end of his blade, then dropped heavily to the ground like a marionette whose strings had been suddenly severed.

Wilkins turned to look at the others, who gazed back at him with conflicting emotions. He'd saved their lives, but he'd also just hacked down the commanding officer who'd led them into and safely out of many a nightmarish scrape over the months they'd been under his charge. Wilkins completely appreciated the enormity of what he'd just done.

'We have no choice in this, men. As I said, failure is not an option. And if I or indeed any one of us should become infected like the poor lieutenant, then I expect each of you to fight to be the one who ends the poor bugger's infernal existence. Do I make myself clear?'

'Yes, sir.'

AT THE AIRFIELD

There'd been an uncomfortable delay whilst they'd waited for the inevitable attack, but within minutes the dead had begun to slowly come at them from all directions at once, crawling out of the forest with a nonchalant lack of speed but unquestionable intent.

The company medic was still trying to do what he could for Private Willard; badly burned, shaking furiously with shock, not long for this world. They'd moved him to the hangar building while the rest of the men formed a defensive line around the top of the airfield. 'This ain't good,' Captain Hunter said to Sergeant Hennessy.

'We can hold them back, sir,' Hennessy was quick to reply. He was spoiling for a fight, desperate to get his teeth into these damn creatures.

'I've no doubt, Sergeant, but that's only half the battle. We're light on supplies and they've got us backed into a corner. It's not just about holding them back, we've got to beat them back too so the airfield's clear for pick-up. We don't know how many of them are out there, and I don't need to remind you, if we don't do what we've been sent here to do, we ain't going home in the morning, understand?'

'Yessir.'

'Tell your men to hit 'em hard in the head. Only use bullets if they have to. Keep the noise down and keep an eye on our ammo.'

'Yessir,' he said again, before saluting and returning to the fray.

Between fifteen and twenty of them were heading straight up the airstrip in an unruly pack. Some of the troops had armed themselves with things they'd scavenged from the airfield to use as bludgeons. Anyone watching would have thought they'd stumbled upon a moonlit gang-fight, a street-corner brawl. The prospect of fighting one-on-one like this (actually more like one-on-many) appealed to some of the men. Better to be bare-knuckle scrapping than sitting waiting like they had been.

And so it began.

Brutal and relentless.

Sergeant Hennessy held back at first, but the adrenalin and fear kicked in and before long he was running at the creatures that shambled towards them. He had a length of metal pipe in his hand that he'd taken from the ruin of the booby-trapped building, and he took great pleasure in using it. He swung it like a sword, and damn near removed the head of the nearest cadaver. 'Take them out,' he ordered his men. 'Take them *all* out. Leave nothing standing.'

INSIDE POLONEZKÖY
FOUR HOURS UNTIL RENDEZVOUS

They used kerosene from one of the lamps and torched the hut they'd been sheltering in, at the same time cremating the body of Lieutenant Henshaw. They took his weapons and kit, and Wilkins collected his identity tags and papers and a photograph and letter from his sweetheart which he found in the dead man's inside pocket. He made a silent promise to himself that when all this was said and done, he'd seek the woman out and tell her what a key role her lost love had played in saving the world. Hollow words, he knew, but he hoped they'd help ease the pain on some level.

The flames from the hut had the desired effect. As the British soldiers snuck out through the rear of the building, the incandescent bloom acted like a call to the faithful, drawing out vast swathes of undead creatures from every corner of the camp. They swarmed like ants over picnic food, competing with each other to get closer to the fire, oblivious to the devastating effect the flames had on both living and dead flesh alike. Jones watched with disbelief from a gap between two other buildings as several of the damn things continued to move, still walking even as their bodies burned. Prisoner and guard alike, all the former barriers of race and rank had been erased by this despicable condition. Nazi, Jew, man, woman, adult, child, captor, captive... now they were all just *the dead*.

This next group of buildings where the four soldiers now found themselves were, thankfully, far more innocuous than the last. By peering in through the dust and grime covered windows, Barton saw that these large, warehouse-like places appeared to be some kind of factory. Although much was hidden by the darkness, the outline of row after row after row of workbenches stretched back into the gloom. Their purpose appeared almost industrial by design. 'Munitions,' Wilkins told him. 'Although my sources suggested a change of design had been mooted for the weapons made here.'

'How so, Lieutenant?'

'We were led to believe that the Nazis intended harvesting the germ and loading it onto their weapons. Rockets and other such. It doesn't bear thinking about, does it?'

'Good grief. You mean Jerry was planning to fire the germ straight at us?'

'Yes. And if you needed any indication of the seriousness of our predicament, which I'm sure you don't, remember that the Nazis appear to have so far resisted doing so. I wonder if the Reich have begun to realise the full implications of what they've created.'

'Strikes me as inhuman that anyone – Nazi or otherwise – could even contemplate using a weapon like this,' Harris said, the disgust in his voice barely concealed.

'War makes good men do awful things, don't ever forget that,' Wilkins warned.

'Our boys would never stoop so low,' Harris said.

'Be under no illusions, if we're not successful in stopping this deadly infection, something far worse may be unleashed. You heard Colonel Adams' warning.'

The endless parade of the burning dead was strangely hypnotising, but the men knew they needed to focus on the task at hand. 'Any sign of Sergeant Steele?' Jones wondered.

'Nothing,' Harris said. 'Not a peep.'

'We can't afford to wait,' Wilkins said. 'We must keep moving.'

Schematics of the concentration camp had been hard to come by, but it seemed likely their instincts were right. The scientist and his laboratory would almost certainly be found in the fortress-like castle at the entrance to Polonezköy – inevitably the hardest part of the camp for them to breach. Built several hundred years ago, it looked as strong and impenetrable as ever. The towering building appeared, from this angle anyway, to be a motley collection of disparate parts: square towers with spires butted up against circular towers which stretched up into the dark sky. Endless grey stone walls seemed to wrap around each other like a maze. And yet there had to be a way in. For the castle to play a functioning part in the day to day operation of the concentration camp, there had to be a number of ways in and out.

'Should we split up?' Harris asked.

'I think it's better we stick together, until we're inside at least,' Barton said quickly.

The men moved across the courtyard at speed, ducking and swerving to avoid more meandering corpses which, for now, were still gravitating towards the light from the fire. They were soon pressed up against the castle wall. Jones looked directly up at the vast keep which towered above him, and froze. 'Not sure if I can do this, sir...' he stammered.

'It's all right to be afraid,' Wilkins told him. 'Between you and me, though, I'd rather be inside with you men for company than left out here on my own, wouldn't you?' He dragged Jones on with him without giving him a chance to renege.

They found a set of steps which sunk down into the ground and ended at a solid-looking door. Wilkins cautiously edged down and listened, but he could hear nothing. He tried the door and found that it opened easily. *Was no door left locked in this bizarre place*, he wondered? He peered inside – seeing nothing initially in the pitch-black – and waited for some kind of response.

'Smells bad,' Jones said from close behind.

Wilkins ducked his head into the doorway and gave out a most un-gentlemanly wolf whistle which was amplified by the acoustics of the ancient building.

'Forgive me, sir, but what the hell are you doing?' Barton asked.

Wilkins didn't have chance to respond, because his call soon had the desired effect. He was immediately aware of movement inside the keep, and he moved out of the way quickly as a surge of dead bodies began to emerge. He found himself trapped at the bottom of the steps by an unexpected (and still growing) number of them and he began hitting out and slashing at them with his knife. Harris came to his rescue, leaning down and yanking him up to safely, a hand under each of his shoulders. He continued to kick out, catching one or two of them, but he needn't have worried because Jones and Barton were already on the case. The advancing corpses seemed unusually dumb and lumbering, perhaps confused by the sudden escape and the shift from inside to outside. Between them they picked seven of them off with the bayonets affixed to the ends of their rifles, leaving them in an unruly heap at the bottom of the few stone steps.

Once they were dealt with, the chaotic attack was over.

Wilkins brushed himself down. The men were relatively safe here, hidden by the slope of the ground and a couple more wooden huts. He could see constant movement in the courtyard, but crucially for now, the dead couldn't see him. Regaining his composure after the sudden exertion of the last few minutes, he took a step forward to examine the corpses they'd just felled. 'Shine a torch down here,' he ordered, and Jones obliged. 'All German,' Wilkins announced. They were all wearing Nazi uniforms and had real weight and bulk to their bodies. A stark contrast with what they'd seen of the prisoner population of the camp so far; cruelly starved and forced to work until their bodies resembled skeletons held together with the merest amount of flesh and sinew.

'There's something different about these,' Barton said, and he hefted one of the corpses to the top of the steps and dumped it on the ground. Jones nearly emptied his stomach when he shone his light into the foul thing's repulsive face. It was far more decayed than any of the other corpses they'd seen since reaching the camp. The skin was heavily discoloured. Wilkins forced himself to get closer to the repugnant aberration. He took its gloved right hand in his and began to bend and flex the arm repeatedly.

'Pardon me, Lieutenant,' Harris said, 'but what in heaven's name are you doing?'

Wilkins said nothing for a few moments longer, his face a picture of concentration. He took off one of his own fingerless gloves and unbuttoned the dead Nazi's heavily stained tunic and shirt. He rested his hand on its pallid skin and agitated it slightly. When he was ready, he answered. 'I'm trying to date the bodies.'

'Date the bodies,' Jones said to the other two. 'What's he on about?'

Wilkins looked up at him disapprovingly. 'If you'd do me the honour of keeping quiet for a short while longer, I'll explain.'

He held open the Nazi's left eye, then prodded its distended belly.

'Come on, sir, I think that's enough...' Barton protested.

Wilkins wiped his hands and stood up. 'It's quite simple really, but important. I've no doubt you've all seen more than your fair share of death since this infernal war began. I've just carried out a few simple tests I've picked up along the way to try and ascertain when a person died. The sclera over the eye, the amount of movement in the joints...'

'Rigor mortis?' Harris suggested.

'That's right. The condition typically manifests itself shortly after death, then relaxes again approximately a day later. Prodding the belly and inspecting the extremities allows me to estimate the gas content of the gut – the longer a person's body has been decaying, the greater the volume of gas produced. Similarly, swollen joints and buttocks can indicate the presence of pools of blood where the corpse has remained in one position for an extended period of time.'

'And rubbing the chest?' Barton asked, curiosity getting the better of him.

'As the body decays and undergoes such dramatic internal changes, so the skin can loosen. I was checking for slippage.'

'So how long have these been dead? And pardon me, Lieutenant, but why in heaven's name does it matter?'

'In answer to your first question, I estimate between three and five days. And with regard to your second point, knowing how long these guards have been dead gives us the best indication we can get as to what has happened here. We know that the prisoners out here are dead, but what about those who were within the castle walls? Did they die first? I have to admit, I believe this place is filled with nothing but death in every conceivable corner. Yet, somewhere in that cesspit of decay, I also believe we might find the secret that will put an end to this nightmare.'

No more talk. Time for action.

Wilkins snapped a branch from a dead tree (*is nothing left alive here?* he wondered) and wrapped a jacket from one of the Nazi corpses around it. He poured lighter fuel over the material then set it ablaze.

The four soldiers ducked down through the low stone doorway and disappeared into the gloom.

INSIDE THE CASTLE

The ancient building was silent, but not quite quiet enough for the soldiers' liking. They had uncovered a complex labyrinth of tunnels beneath the heart of the castle, and despite their best efforts to pass through the place unnoticed, the noise their every move made seemed to be amplified beyond all proportion. Their boots echoed off the walls, every step like a gunshot, and even the sounds of their breathing seemed to fill the air with noise. Wilkins took the lead carrying the flaming torch while Harris brought up the rear. The passages they moved along were claustrophobic and tight: dark grey walls, low curved ceiling, dripping damp, a layer of slurry underfoot.

It wasn't long before they were under attack again.

A sudden sharp right turn led to another long corridor which seemed to stretch the entire length of the castle. It was so long that the light from Wilkins' torch barely reached halfway, and it was only when the flickering shadows began to move towards them that the British soldiers realised more of the enemy were close at hand. Three more Nazi corpses came at them suddenly as if they'd been woken from hibernation by the unannounced arrival of the Brits. Their faces, withered and drawn into furious expressions of anger and hatred, appeared infinitely more hideous in the wavering light. Barton, now unfazed and increasingly confident when facing the dead, carefully pushed past Wilkins and dealt with all three of the dead Germans in quick succession. He thrust his bayonet through the left eye of the nearest at the same time as dragging the second one down then planting his boot between its shoulder blades. He slid the first creature off his blade, then drove the sharp point up through the chin of the next into what remained of its putrefying brain. Barton finally returned his attention to the ghoul at his feet which he spiked angrily through the back of the head with far more aggression than was necessary.

'You looked as if you almost enjoyed that,' Harris said from the rear.

'I did,' Barton replied. 'These things are miserably weak—'

'—yet incredibly dangerous,' Wilkins warned, 'and we'd all do well to remember that. One scratch is all it might take to spread the condition. One bite. Remember, that's what did it for Lieutenant Henshaw.'

And the men became silent at the memory of their recently fallen officer.

'Keep moving,' Jones said, his voice little more than a whisper. 'Let's get this done and get home.'

Wilkins checked his watch. Under four hours to go.

They'd realised what they were likely to find down here long before they reached it. The castle keep. Most of the dungeon-like cells were being used for storage (and they took the welcome opportunity to arm themselves when it presented itself), yet other rooms clearly had a purpose more akin to their originally intended use. 'No sense locking people up in here,' Barton had observed. 'Not when this whole bloody place is a prison.'

They'd thought nothing of his words until they'd reached the third cell along. Each of these confined chambers was claustrophobically small. The rough walls, hewn from centuries-old rock, were thicker than a man's arm and the portcullis-like iron doors appeared virtually impenetrable.

Thankfully.

In the third cell was a cadaver so badly decayed that, at first sight, the men had difficulty recognising it as being human. It was naked, and its discoloured flesh was covered in a layer of dried blood, glistening decay and other, less obvious grime. The floor was awash with seepage and putrescent dribbles. The creature threw itself at the railings when the men neared, and though it was initially held back by shackles and chains, the force with which it lunged was such that one arm was wrenched out of its socket. The stump twitched furiously. 'What happened to it?' Jones asked. The smell here was suffocating, like nothing he'd ever endured before.

Harris used the butt of his rifle to shove the monstrous thing back, and it tripped over what was left of its own feet, ending up in the far corner of the cell, thrashing furiously in its own mire but quite unable to pick itself back up and come at the men again.

Wilkins braved the stench and the creature's fury to get closer. He raised the torch to get a better view, though at the back of his mind was the concern that had the gases generated as a result of this thing's decomposition not yet fully dissipated, he might ignite an explosive cloud of noxious odour. He covered his mouth and nose and peered into the gloom, only stepping back when he could stand to see no more. 'I believe this must be one of the very first of them. I presume this is all that remains of one of the scientists' earliest experiments.'

'Why keep it locked up?' Barton asked. 'Why not just get rid of it?'

'I assume they were studying it. By keeping it isolated down here, away from everyone else, they might have been hoping to observe its behaviour and condition.'

'You think it did all this to itself?'

'Almost certainly. The natural process of decay is responsible for much of what you can see here, but the effects have been magnified by the inherent fury of the beast. Remember, these things are only able to reason at the most basic of levels. They are only interested in fighting. Self-preservation is an unknown concept to them. That's if their brains are even capable of considering concepts.'

'You've lost me again,' Barton said. 'Pardon me, Lieutenant Wilkins, but you have a frustrating habit of using a hundred words where one or two would probably do.'

'He's saying that because this thing was locked away, it tore itself apart,' Harris explained.

'Then that's a good thing, isn't it?' asked Jones. 'Won't they all end up like this then? Or they'll all rot down to nothing at least.'

'That may be so,' Wilkins said, 'but it'll take time. And as long as they're left to their own devices out there, they'll continue to kill and to multiply. It makes them even more of a threat, not less. Can't you see, they'll stop at nothing to spread this infernal condition around the globe. *Nothing*!'

The group moved on, leaving the furious inhuman beast eviscerating itself on the cold stone floor of its cell.

Steps. Another heavy wooden door.

'Thank the lord,' Wilkins said under his breath, and he allowed himself to lower the flaming torch at last. His arm ached with the effort of keeping it aloft, but he hadn't dared not use it. The corridors under the castle were like a maze. It wouldn't have taken much for them to lose all sense of direction and keep going around in circles.

Harris went to start climbing, but Wilkins stopped him. 'Come on, sir, the sooner we get on with this the better. I can't stand all this waiting around. If there's going to be a fight, then let's get fighting and let's get home. All this talk of deadly germs and super-weapons is just making matters worse.'

'We need to keep our wits about us,' Wilkins warned. 'If there are any Nazis left in this building – dead or alive – they'll be gunning for us. We can be assured of a pretty grim welcome, whoever and whatever we find up those stairs.'

He was right, of course, and no one argued. Wilkins climbed to the top of the stairs and readied himself. He glanced across at Harris who nodded to show that he was ready, then opened the door.

Both men recoiled when a shocking number of large brown and black rats scurried through the suddenly open doorway and flooded down the stairs, a tidal wave of dirty fur and yellowed teeth. At the bottom of the steps, Jones' nerve almost broke. He aimed his weapon into the undulating mass crawling hurriedly over and around his boots. 'Hold your fire,' Wilkins ordered. Jones' finger tightened on the trigger, but he didn't shoot.

'I hate rats,' he grumbled, watching them surge down the corridor, looking like a bizarrely undulating carpet. Squeaks of fear and spiny, lashing tails.

'They're clearly not interested in us, are they?' Wilkins said. 'They're leaving the proverbial sinking ship.'

Barton took hold of Jones' collar and turned the young soldier to face him. 'Look at me, Jones.'

'Get off.'

'Not until you calm yourself down, lad. The rats are the least of our problems. You need to forget about them and focus on whatever it is they're running away from.'

Eventually the steps became clear, and Wilkins and Harris went through the door into the main part of the castle. They were surprised to find that there was some illumination here. Electric lamps which glowed dull yellow were strung along the wall like fading Christmas lanterns. Wilkins extinguished the torch and tossed it aside. He felt infinitely better carrying a pistol in one hand and his trusty knife in the other. Holding the flame had hampered his ability to defend and attack.

Although still uncomfortably quiet, after the cramped confines of the level below-ground, the increased space up here felt strangely liberating. No more stooping. The ceilings were high. No longer enclosed by unending solid walls on either side. Space to move. Options. And yet, despite its size, the whole place felt foetid and filthy. There were marks and smears everywhere they looked. Bloody handprints. Drag marks. Drips and pools of crimson gore.

They moved as a pack along the wide corridor, covering all angles between them. The first doorway they came across led into a large kitchen, and they entered to briefly stop and take stock. Food had been left half-prepared and unattended on counters and stoves. There were several large cooking pots, the unidentifiable contents of which had been baked solid. The flesh of a pig on a spit was black and hardened. Wilkins checked the enormous oven at the centre of the kitchen. 'No residual heat,' he said. 'This oven's as cold as this poor unfortunate soul.' He nodded at the body of a woman slumped in a corner of the room. She wore a simple grey pinafore dress which was heavily stained with blood from what was left of her head. It also covered much of the wall behind her. She appeared to have been shot at extraordinarily close range, and Wilkins wondered if she'd perhaps done this to herself to escape whatever nightmare had unfolded around her.

The only sound in the kitchen came from dripping taps and dripping blood, but they could clearly hear noises coming from elsewhere in the castle. Barton led them back out into the corridor, but soon found that he could go no further. There was a blockage up ahead. A heavy piece of antique-looking furniture had been pulled away from the wall and dragged across a doorway. 'We've no option but to keep going, far as I can see,' he said, and Wilkins agreed. They could hear movement on the other side of the door which increased in frequency and volume when Barton spoke.

'Do it,' Lieutenant Wilkins ordered.

The men took up position back along the corridor and Barton began to move the dresser. The fury of the dead was incredible. They hammered against the door to get through, and the sheer force of the weight of dead flesh pushing forward was such that by the time Barton had shifted the dresser just a few inches, the first few grabbing hands were shoved through the gap, reaching out for him and his colleagues. Harris ran forward and began hacking at them with his bayonet, intent on doing as much damage as possible before they were released. Flesh was slashed, bones were broken, and hands and fingers were sliced off, but the dead continued to fight undeterred.

Another brutal shove forward from the other side.

The heavy oak dresser was shunted back another six inches, leaving almost enough of a gap for the first cadaver to get through. It was the reanimated body of another SS- Totenkopfverbände guard, replete in its blood-drenched uniform, tunic still done up to the neck, silver buttons shining brightly amidst the gore. The vicious creature appeared to be straining to get through, but it quickly became clear that it was trapped, snagged on the door, and was being pushed forward by the force of other ghouls trying to get through from behind. Harris came at the monster again, this time stabbing it through its clouded right eye and doing enough damage to immediately extinguish all aggression and render the corpse completely useless. It dropped heavily, but even before it had hit the ground it had been shoved out of the way by more of the rabid dead surging forward. With no communication between them, just a terrifying, unspoken desire, they pushed the door open further and another two broke through. Harris gestured for the others to stay back. 'I've got this. No point us all getting our kit grubby.'

He managed the faintest of laughs, but all thoughts of humour disappeared in a heartbeat. As he leaned forward to dispatch another of the hellish monstrosities, a rogue hand reached through the half-open door and grabbed hold of his over-jacket. He didn't notice at first, so distracted was he by the vile soldier writhing at his feet which he kicked repeatedly in the face. Harris' momentary delay in reacting enabled another one of the corpses to snag a loop of his belt with several rotting fingers.

And then another caught him.

Then another.

And another.

It happened so fast that there was nothing anyone could do. The smell of fresh blood seemed to drive the already wild crowd into an utter frenzy, and in seconds even more of them had reached through the gap and taken hold of Harris' clothing and kit. He tried to fight back, but it was already too late. The more he fought, the tighter their grip on him became.

Barton, Wilkins and Jones rushed to help their colleague, but there was little they could do. Wilkins and Jones were caught up with other dead soldiers which had managed to squeeze through the gap. Jones tried to re-kill one of them which towered over him, but its frantic movements were so unpredictable that whenever he thought he had a clear chance of shoving his bayonet into its skull, it either moved or managed to push the barrel of his rifle away.

By the time he'd dealt with it and the others had managed to wipe up the other stragglers who'd broken through, it was too late.

Harris screamed as a smaller corpse, that of an imprisoned child, sank its yellowed teeth into the exposed flesh on the back of one of his hands. 'Bastard!' he screamed, and he dropped his rifle with the pain, then instinctively reached for the pistol he carried holstered on his belt.

'No, Harris, don't!' Wilkins yelled, but it was too late.

Harris was a seething mass of grabbing hands now. It looked like there were hundreds of them pulling at his body, trying to drag him closer to their snapping mouths and deadly germs, but somehow he managed to make a half-turn to face his attackers and began firing indiscriminately into the writhing, squirming mass. The noise riled the despicable crowd to new heights, causing them to push harder and harder until the door was completely open.

Harris was swallowed up. At the last possible moment he slipped the pistol into his mouth and pulled the trigger. The back of his skull exploded outwards, showering Jones and the others. The young soldier stood his ground for a moment, too stunned to move, but the sight of the dead crawling over his colleague's fallen corpse was enough to force him into action. 'Run!' he screamed. 'Just run!'

The three remaining Brits sprinted back the way they'd just come, pursued by a slow yet unstoppable tsunami of the dead.

Jones hurtled past the kitchen door. Wilkins shot out an arm and pulled him back. 'In here, lad. Quick.'

'We need to get out of this place.'

'No, Jones, we need to find the scientist.'

'The lieutenant's right,' Barton said as he shut the door behind the other two. 'After what just happened to Harris, there's no way I'm going to let those damn things win.'

'But the kitchen's a dead end,' Jones protested.

Barton shoved Jones out of the way. 'Help me block the door, Lieutenant.'

Wilkins grunted with effort as he began to push a heavy table across the stone floor towards the door.

Barton held it shut for as long as he could, then moved at the last possible moment. The dead army was already outside; he could hear them and feel them as they fought to gain access. Jones' fear seemed suddenly to imbue him with superhuman strength and, like a man possessed, he snapped out of his malaise and helped shove the table into position then stack more kitchen furniture against it. The dead were hammering to get at them now but, for the moment, the door was holding fast.

'They'll get through eventually, won't they?' Jones said, watching the door as it rattled in its frame.

Wilkins was quick to reassure him. 'There's far less space out there. The last door was at the end of the corridor, not halfway along it. They'll struggle to get enough numbers and weight behind them to push their way through.'

'You sure about that?'

'As sure as I can be.'

'That means no, he isn't,' Barton added unhelpfully.

The three comrades stepped back from the door and waited nervously, panting hard with the effort of their exertion.

A pause.

A brief moment to collect breath and compose thoughts.

Six men down to three, Wilkins thought, *and we're no closer to finding Doctor Månsson.*

'About that wooden thing that was blocking the last door,' Jones said.

'What about it?' asked Wilkins.

'How did it get there?'

'What kind of a ridiculous question is that? How am I supposed to know?'

'I think it's a very sensible question,' Barton announced, siding with Jones. 'Think about it, Lieutenant. Someone moved it from this side, they must have. But as far as we know, the only way of getting to it was the route we took to get in here.'

'Then maybe it was that poor wretch,' Wilkins suggested, gesturing at the cook's headless corpse in the corner.

'I don't reckon you're right. She don't look like she had the strength, and where's the weapon she used to kill herself? And why would she kill herself just after she's got safe?'

'There could be any number of reasons...'

'Granted, but I don't reckon she did it. I reckon it was someone else.'

'So where are they?'

'My question exactly. Either they're in here with us, or there's another way out of this kitchen.'

The three British soldiers immediately began to investigate their surroundings more closely. The vast kitchen was ice-cold and as silent as the grave and, apart from the solitary corpse they'd found previously, the place appeared completely empty. There were windows, but they had been covered with metal bars from outside, presumably to keep the prisoners working in the kitchen safely locked-up inside.

A heavy curtain hung along one wall. Barton looked under either end and found a discreet doorway which led into a narrow pantry. The shelves had already been largely cleared, but it wasn't the supplies that interested Barton. Instead, he was intent on tracing a route through the mess he'd found there. It looked like someone had tried to effect an escape, using shelving stacked against one wall, but where had they gone? The light was virtually non-existent in here, and he was having trouble making sense of it all.

'Here, let me,' Jones said, and he squeezed past Barton to get through. Barton helped himself to an apple as he watched Jones explore, the little man's movements hard to discern in the gloom.

'He was a proper little tea-leaf, by all accounts,' he said to Wilkins who was now standing just behind him. 'Been straightened out by the war, has Jones.'

'Then let's hope he can find us a way out of here,' Wilkins said quietly, feeling his way along the shelves to his right. He found this an awfully depressing place. The body of the woman upstairs, combined with Harris' unnecessary death, had affected him quite badly. The cruelty of Polonezköy appeared to know no bounds, and they were yet to find the cold heart of this place. He dared not imagine what would be waiting for them there. For now he occupied himself with thoughts of the prisoners forced to work in this kitchen; preparing feasts for their captors whilst they themselves starved. This war was inhuman on so many different levels...

'Got it!' Jones announced from up high. 'There's a window up here. It's not huge, so you might have a problem getting your belly through it, Barton.'

'Watch yourself, Jones,' he warned.

'Looks like someone covered it from outside once they'd got through.'

'Then let us get through and we'll see if we can find them,' Wilkins said. 'Lead the way.'

Jones did as he was told, and after much wriggling and holding of breath, he was soon through and standing on the other side. The window, although high on the pantry wall, was only just above ground level. He found himself in an enclosed courtyard about the size of half a football pitch.

'Give us a hand, Jones,' Barton hissed, and Jones obliged and helped pull his colleague through the narrow window and out into the open. Wilkins passed Barton's kit through, then his own, then climbed through himself.

'Well done, Jones,' he said. 'Where now?'

They were looking around for doorways and passages, when someone whistled from across the way. Barton looked up and saw a light flashing in a window halfway up a tower directly opposite them. There was a door at the bottom of the tower which he moved quickly towards.

'Careful, Barton, it might be a trap,' Jones said.

'I'd have expected Jerry to take pot-shots at us rather than invite us up for a chat, wouldn't you?'

He led the others up a short staircase, his rifle held ready, just in case.

'It's about time you chaps turned up,' an instantly familiar voice said. It was Sergeant Steele. He was sitting on a landing, eating a veritable feast he'd half-hitched from the kitchen on his way through. He offered his food and drink to the others.

'How the devil did you get here?' Wilkins asked.

'I'm guessing you three found another way into the castle. I'm afraid I inadvertently blocked the passage I found.'

'We had noticed.'

'I managed to get myself followed by more than a few of those damn things but I outsprinted them and was able to stop them getting through. I found myself in the kitchens and looked for another way out. I didn't much fancy trying to descend any deeper. Not alone, anyway.'

'A wise move,' Wilkins said.

'I thought I should stay put. This tower's relatively central, and there doesn't seem to be as many of them around here. I wondered if you'd find my escape route. Where's Harris, by the way?'

Jones shook his head sadly. Steele nodded, but said nothing. Harris wasn't the first colleague he'd lost, and he knew he'd almost certainly not be the last.

'I take it you've done a recce?' Wilkins asked. 'Is there a way out, or are we trapped here?'

'Oh, we're not trapped,' Steele told him. 'But we might as well be.'

THE AIRFIELD AT LEGINÓW

The bodies were mounting up.

Less than forty troops had brought down treble that number of advancing undead creatures. They were finally starting to thin out, stumbling onto the airfield in dribs and drabs now. Some were little more than withered husks, the reanimated remains of locals. Others, however, had once been soldiers, and despite having lost every shred of humanity, the urge to maim and to kill remained. They dragged themselves along until they saw one of the Americans when the scent of the living seemed to reinvigorate them, transforming them from mindless shambling shells to brutal killers in seconds.

Half of Captain Hunter's men were still fighting back their unnatural attackers, the other half removing the debris of battle from the airfield. Men moved quickly in pairs, picking up corpses by the hands and feet, then carrying them over to near the hangar and leaving them in a pile. Hunter thought he'd like to torch the grotesque mound and keep throwing more and more of the bastards on top of the heap, but the flames would inevitably attract even more of them.

Sergeant Hennessy was unrecognisable. Dripping with blood. Panting with effort. Steam rose from his sweat-soaked body. 'I think we're there, Captain,' he said, breathless.

'I think you're right, Hennessy. Clear the decks, hold the perimeter, and keep the damn noise down.'

IN THE HEART OF THE CASTLE
TWO HOURS UNTIL RENDEZVOUS

Steele had explored the tower while he'd been waiting for the others. His logic had been sound: from his relatively central vantage point he would have been able to see them coming from various angles, and having the benefit of the high ground meant he would have been able to defend himself had the need arisen.

'If the scientist is still alive, I think I know where he is,' he explained as he led the others deeper into the castle.

'Are you sure this is safe?' Wilkins asked as they climbed more steps.

'As sure as I can be. I've not yet come across any of the dead this high. That's not to say they won't be up here, so keep your wits about you. This is just about the vilest place on Earth, from what I've seen of it, sir.'

At the top of the staircase, Steele took them out through a door and onto a short walkway which connected this tower to another identical one, either side of the main entrance. The wind up here was bracing, and carried with it sounds of fighting in the distance. 'Captain Hunter and his men?' asked Jones.

'I assume so,' Wilkins replied. 'Damnation. It sounds like they're having as torrid a time as we are.'

'Then let's keep moving, Lieutenant,' Steele said. 'Time is most definitely of the essence tonight.'

Jones hesitated. 'Wait... Listen...'

'What is it, Jones?'

'More of the dead, I think. Down below us.'

He was right. The men peered down over the battlements. From here they could see the edge of another vast area of the camp. More dead soldiers and prisoners were gravitating towards it. 'Where are they all heading?' Barton asked.

'Come with me and all will be revealed,' Steele told them. 'But brace yourselves. The news isn't good.'

They entered the next tower, and Barton immediately primed his weapon to fire. He could hear the dead. And they were close.

'Arm yourselves, men,' Wilkins ordered.

'Please... just wait,' Steele said. 'It's perfectly safe.'

'Nothing in this place is safe at all,' Wilkins angrily corrected him. Steele beckoned for the others to follow. A spiral staircase led down into the dark depths.

'Shine your torch down there, Jones,' Steele said, and Jones did as instructed. 'It's all right. They're not getting up this way.'

Jones nervously edged further and further down, then stopped when he saw it. A semi-solid mass of writhing flesh, like a scab blocking the stairs. An apparently endless number of bodies had become entangled and had formed an impenetrable blockage, no way up or down. Steele had made things certain by dropping furniture on top of them. Chairs. A desk. The staircase was permanently out of action, but there was clearly no way the dead would get through. Disfigured faces stared up at Jones from deep within the horrific mess. Dead eyes filled with desperation to get at him, and fury because they were trapped.

'Where now?' Wilkins asked.

'This way,' Steele answered, and the three men followed him into what was, unmistakably, a laboratory. It was like nothing any of them had seen before. A hellish place, the bloody remnants of abandoned experiments lay everywhere. 'Don't touch anything,' Steele warned. 'The entire place is almost certainly contagious.'

At one end of the room was a grey, bullet-marked wall which had been drenched with numerous splashes and fountains of blood. Nearby, parts of eviscerated cadavers still lay strapped to metal trollies and tables. Much of the medical equipment appeared to have been smashed to pieces and lay in ruin all around them.

'So it seems our Doctor Månsson may have been a victim of his own creations,' Wilkins said, surmising from the chaos.

'That's what I thought at first,' Steele replied. 'I think there's more to it than that, though.'

'Really?'

'Yes. Take a closer look. Much of this equipment has been deliberately wrecked. From what we've seen of the dead, would they really be interested in doing anything like this? Electrical equipment has been smashed, the innards torn out. All these test tubes and phials... there's not a single one that's been left undamaged. No, gentleman, I believe this laboratory has been systematically destroyed, perhaps by the doctor himself.'

'And what about Månsson?'

'It's my belief that he's being held hostage, if he's still alive that is.'

'By whom?'

'By the last Nazis left alive in this godforsaken place, that's who. Allow me to show you.'

Sergeant Steele doubled-back and exited the laboratory, then followed another passageway which led in the opposite direction. They were now on the easternmost edge of the ancient building, overlooking a vast swathe of Polonezköy which had, until now, remained largely unseen. The four soldiers peered down through narrow slits in the stonework.

'Good Lord,' Wilkins gasped.

'Bloody hell,' Barton cursed. 'You reckon our man's in the middle of that lot?'

'If he's anywhere at all, yes.'

Below the east wall of the castle, stretching out all the way to the wall running around the entire perimeter of the concentration camp site, was a crowd of bodies the likes of which none of them had ever seen – nor had ever wanted to see – before. It reminded Wilkins of movie-reel footage he'd seen of Hitler's Nuremberg rallies: an apparently endless sea of heads, all crowding together in a show of slavish devotion. Unlike those Nazi events, however, the crowd here behaved entirely differently.

Less a crowd, more a swarm.

Nazis, prisoners, men, women and children...

Hundreds. *Thousands.*

Dead. Every last one of them.

When flocking to hear the Fuhrer speak, the faithful (or fearful, or both) remained largely stationary to listen and observe. Here, the vast numbers of people pushed ever closer to something just left of centre of the immense gathering. At first Wilkins couldn't make out what it was he was looking at, but then the details began to come into focus.

There were a number of buildings in the midst of the chaos. Some had clearly already been overrun by the enemy: doors hanging open, crammed with corpses trying to get in whilst others forced their way out. The movement of the rotting masses around these wooden huts appeared strangely like eddies in white-water flows, turning in on themselves again and again, many of the creatures being dragged underfoot and being trampled by many, many more.

But there remained one building which was resolutely closed-up. It was also the one which appeared to be attracting the most attention from the decaying hordes. Steele saw that his colleagues had identified it as quickly as he had. 'If our scientist chappie is still alive, I'll wager that's where he'll be. Right in the middle of all that damned mess.'

'Then we might as well give up and get out of this hellish place right now,' Jones said.

'We can't do that and you know it, Jones,' Wilkins snapped at him. 'Good Lord, man, do I really have to remind you again what's at stake here?'

'No, sir, you don't, you've already told me enough times and I know it anyway. But that don't change anything. I don't see how we're going to get anyone out of that mess down there alive.'

'It gets worse,' Steele said.

'How can this get any worse?'

'If Doctor Månsson is down there, then he's not alone. I believe he has plenty of company in that building, both Nazi and civilian.'

'Why would the Nazis allow prisoners in there with them?' Jones asked, perfectly sensibly.

'Collateral,' Wilkins answered quickly. 'It makes sense. They're desperate – desperate to survive and desperate to get out alive. There's a perfectly good reason for them to keep hold of the doctor and any number of prisoners too. The doctor would be a bargaining chip, because I'm sure his significance to our side won't have gone unnoticed.'

'And the civilians?'

'A cushion, if you will. A safety net between either us and them or, more likely, between Jerry and the dead.'

'Way I see it, we'll struggle to get anyone out of there,' Barton said, sounding increasingly dejected.

'We can do it,' Wilkins said, eternally optimistic. 'I have an idea.'

'Excuse me, sir,' Jones said, 'but we've less than two hours and...'

'And what, Lance Corporal?'

'And there's likely to be quite a number of Nazis down there along with several thousand or more of those horrible dead things. What hope do the four of us have against all of them?'

'You're absolutely right, soldier. That's why we need to take a different tack and even out the odds. We need to get the dead working for us.'

OVERLOOKING THE DEAD
ONE HOUR UNTIL RENDEZVOUS

'**This is never** going to work, Sarge,' Barton whispered secretively to Steele, keeping his voice low for fear of being overheard by the lieutenant.

'For all our sakes we'd better hope it does.'

Wilkins sensed their unease. 'I'm sure I know what you're whispering about, chaps, but I need you to have a little faith. I've done something like this previously.'

'We do have a little faith in you, Lieutenant. Problem is, right now it is just a little...'

Jones looked up from his work and watched nervously for Lieutenant Wilkins' reaction to that. He'd have laughed out loud himself if he hadn't been so damn frightened.

'You're really going to do this?' Barton asked. Wilkins nodded.

'I don't believe I have any choice. And I certainly wouldn't ask any of you fellows to do something I wasn't prepared to do myself.'

'Then good luck to you, sir.'

He stepped forward and the two men shook hands.

'And to you too, Barton. Now, you all know what I need each of you to do?'

'We know what to do, but we're not sure about *when*. Will you give us some kind of signal?'

'You won't need a signal, believe me. Now I'll wish you all well and I'll be on my way. I'll see you back at the rendezvous point in little under an hour.'

And with that, he was gone.

Wilkins was soon outside again.

It felt good to be beyond the imposing enclosure of the castle walls, but unnerving to be out in the open again like this. No cover. No defence. Just him, a handful of Nazis, and the entire remaining undead population of the Polonezköy prison camp.

He'd retraced his steps as best he could, weighed down with the necessary supplies they'd half-hitched from the cellars earlier. Once he'd reached the small enclosed courtyard where Steele had found them, he'd used the grappling hook to scale the castle wall and climb down into the main part of the camp again.

The sun was about to rise. It would be daylight soon: a relentless countdown. If Captain Hunter and his men had managed to hold the airfield, how long would they wait? Every second mattered now. Wilkins knew he was working against an unstoppable clock. It felt like this was an impossible task.

Keep moving.

Never stop.

He had only to remember the responsibility which rested on his shoulders to know that he had no choice. He simply had to keep going.

He used the burned out hut where Lieutenant Henshaw had met his unfortunate end as a marker, then looked up to try and make out the walkway between the castle towers from which he'd observed the direction of the dead a short time earlier. There were only occasional bodies here, and they appeared to have as little interest in him as he had in them. They were distracted instead by the low noise coming from the massive crowd to the east. Although singularly quiet, the cumulative noise was again extraordinary. Thousands upon thousands of slothful, dragging footsteps.

And it was closer to the repellent crowd that he now forced himself to move. Tucked in tight against the castle wall again, he crept slowly around until he found himself mingling with the fringes of the undead hordes; as near as he could get to the festering masses without becoming part of the crowd.

Here goes nothing, he thought. Then he stopped and corrected himself. *Here goes* everything.

Wilkins pulled the pins of grenade after grenade after grenade and hurled them as far as he could towards the outermost part of the crowd. The first explosion came in seconds, sending bodies flying in all directions, and at the same time causing huge swathes of the dead to surge towards the sudden disturbance, more of them starting to move with each subsequent blast. Their interest in the chaos allowed him to move with a little more freedom and he moved deeper into their number. Using the first detonations as a marker point – similar, he smiled to himself, to when he and the boys played darts in the squadron social club – this time he shifted his aim slightly to ensure the next munitions he threw exploded alongside the outer wall.

In the split-second flash of one powerful ignition he saw that he'd successfully punched a hole through the wall, then he threw several more grenades to make that hole larger still.

Was it his imagination, or was the light improving more quickly than he'd expected? Did he have even less time than he'd originally thought?

In the brief gaps between explosions, he'd thought he'd heard voices. Now he could hear them clearly. It was the Nazis in the hut at the centre of the chaos fighting amongst themselves. Squabbling. Arguing. Some panicking because they thought they were under attack, others doing everything they could to keep the noise down because they recognised the effect it would have on the hungry dead outside.

To Wilkins' immense relief, however, the first part of his plan appeared to be working. The majority of the dead were continuing to move away from the Germans and towards the epicentre of the blasts. 'One more for luck,' he said quietly to himself, and he lobbed his penultimate grenade through the air. This one landed on the edge of the advancing crowd and blew scores more of the abhorrent creatures to kingdom come.

If the Nazis were watching him and trying to follow his plan, he thought, his next move would throw them into even more confusion.

Rather than heading straight for the Germans in the hut, he instead ran in the opposite direction towards the hole in the outer wall. He was moving in the same direction as the dead, but with far more speed and control, and though the ground was increasingly uneven – littered with craters and lumps of burning flesh – his progress was largely unimpeded. A stormtrooper corpse managed to wrap one decaying hand around his arm as he tried to side-step it, but his speed was such that it couldn't keep its balance and it fell. Wilkins found himself dragging the ghoul behind. Its grip on his sleeve was tenacious, and he resorted to punching it in the face to get rid of it. His hand stung with pain and was drenched with blood and gore.

Made it.

He'd reached the hole in the outer wall, and there he stopped – just for a moment, just long enough to turn back and holler 'Come and get me!'

He waited as long as he dared, enough time to be certain that enough of the dead had seen him and were now following, hopefully starting a chain reaction, before running along the gap between the wall and the electrified fence. He paused and looked back again, long enough this time to be sure his audacious plan was working. The dead appeared to be flooding through the hole he'd made, and at once the air began to fill with sparks and crackles and foul-smelling smoke as cadaver after cadaver collided with the wire-mesh and began to burn. Those which didn't reach the fence were now spilling out in either direction, filling the gap between the wall and the fence.

Wilkins crept back into the courtyard, heading straight for the back of the occupied hut. Several of the Nazis had already emerged from their shelter into the space where the dead had been. A sizeable number of rogue bodies remained close, and the Germans were forced to defend themselves from frequent attacks. Wilkins watched in horror as a screaming prisoner was sacrificed in the vain hope of distracting more of the masses – kicked out into the open and made to run for cover. He'd barely made it twenty yards before he was overcome by corpses, unable to defend himself in his miserably weak, emaciated condition. A lone Obergrenadier stranded near to the hut was also caught out in the open, and another pack descended on him and tore him apart. His screams helped divert more undead attention away from his officers and other remaining countrymen who tried to work out what was happening in the midst of the inexplicable chaos. Watching events unfold from on high, Steele put all but a couple of those he could see out of their misery with quick-fire, well-aimed precision shots from a Mauser Kar 98k they'd taken from the keep.

As a result of Steele's stealthy attack, the remaining Germans retreated back into their hut which was immediately sealed again. Jones and Barton watched events unfold intently, waiting at ground level for Wilkins to give them their signal to move.

One of the Nazis spotted Wilkins as he sprinted towards the lowly building. The German took pot-shots at him from a window and he was forced to zigzag wildly to avoid being hit. He ran straight past the hut and took cover behind another, further confusing the already bemused krauts. Several of them emerged again, only to be driven back by Steele shooting from high in the tower. The soldiers looked up for him, trying to work out the angle of the shot which had taken out their colleagues, then firing up at the castle walls. They missed the window from which Steele had been shooting, but their bullets were close enough to make the Brit pull his head back and duck out of sight.

Their confidence returning, the Nazis stepped further out into the open, but they hadn't reckoned on Barton and Jones and they were brought down by a volley from Jones who came screaming at them from out of nowhere.

No more Germans. Jones peered in through the window, but could see only a mass of prisoners inside. 'All clear,' he shouted to the others.

But it wasn't clear.

Jones threw the door open, only to be mown down by several more Nazis who'd remained inside the hut, hiding amongst their captives. Jones was dead before he hit the ground.

'Bastards!' Barton yelled, giving away his position. He attempted a run on the hut but was driven back by still more gunfire. Wilkins tried to get to him, but he too was under attack the moment he stepped out from cover, and a handful of approaching bodies were also getting too close for comfort.

Up high, Steele tried to make sense of what was happening below him. There was another loud crackle and he saw that the weight of the advancing undead were in the process of bringing a section of the border fence down. They appeared unstoppable from this distance, and when the power to the fence was terminated, there was little left to deter them. The wire-mesh began to bow and sag under their weight, and soon it was low enough for them to trample over and escape out into the wilds. Their progress initially slowed by numbers, many more of the dead had begun to double-back towards the hut again.

'*Schnell, schnell... bekommen die Hölle hier raus!*'

Faced with the imminent return of a sizeable number of the undead hordes, the few remaining Nazis made a run for it. They moved alongside innocent prisoners, using them both as cover and bait. Steele set up the Mauser again, but by the time he was ready to take a shot it was already too late. The captors were indistinguishable from their captives from up here.

He watched as Wilkins emerged from his hiding place and walked out into the open, behind the crowd of prisoners the Nazis were herding towards the castle. 'I say,' he shouted, 'I think you should stop right there. We have you covered from in front, behind and above.' He glanced over his shoulder nervously. Several of the furthest forward dead were heading in his direction, but he stood his ground. He had a few seconds yet. Steele took a couple of the nearest of them out with aces. 'Nice shooting,' Wilkins said under his breath.

'*Britische Abschaum Sie sterben!*' a furious Nazi officer bellowed, and he came at Wilkins with his rifle raised. His British counterpart stood his ground and refused to move. Two more Germans separated from the main group and moved closer, leaving only a couple to corral the remaining prisoners who were gathered in an uncomfortable mass in the middle of a relative ocean of space. The light was definitely improving. Wilkins scanned the crowd and, in the midst of all the faces, he caught sight of one he'd committed to memory. Doctor Egil Månsson. The Swedish scientist looked as terrified as those civilians he now stood alongside. He clutched the hand of a dishevelled little girl who appeared completely traumatised, her face devoid of all emotion.

The Nazi moved towards Wilkins, stopping only when he saw that more of the undead were creeping uncomfortably near, and when he realised that Barton was close at hand with his rifle aimed directly at him. Wilkins noted from his dress that he appeared to be a senior officer.

'I suggest you calm down and listen to me,' Wilkins said. 'Are you in charge here? Rather, were you in charge here?'

'I am Obersturmbannführer Scherler.' His accent was strong, but his English was impeccable.

'Obersturmbannführer, eh? That sounds mighty impressive.'

'I run this camp, you infidel,' Scherler screamed at him.

'Well I hope you don't mind me saying, you've not made that good a job of it.'

'How dare you! I should kill you right now,' the Nazi threatened.

'How tedious. You bloody fool, there are far bigger things at stake here than you and I, do you not understand?'

'Do you really believe any of us will be getting out of here alive?' Scherler replied.

'Yes I do, as it happens, and if you play ball you might make it out of here too. Now if you'll just hand Doctor Månsson over to me I'll...'

The doctor immediately began to protest. Wilkins couldn't make out a damn word he was saying, but he was becoming increasingly agitated. He continued to hold onto the little girl who remained impassive; detached and unemotional. No doubt permanently scarred by the ordeal she'd endured at the hands of the Nazis here at Polonezköy.

A surge of movement from way over to the left of the group distracted Barton. Another herd of corpses, hitherto held back by a wooden gate which had given way and collapsed under their weight, made directly for the British soldier and the crowd of innocents gathered close behind. Barton opened fire on the dead immediately, and whilst many of them were felled, many more were not. The gunfire caused panic among the remaining prisoners and Nazis alike, all of them scattering in every direction like startled sheep. From relative calm to absolute chaos in seconds. The slender advantage Wilkins and the others had fought to gain was immediately undone.

A horrific scream. Over to Wilkins' left, one of the prisoners was brought down by three of the corpses attacking at once.

To his right, a Nazi lay on his belly in the dirt being torn to pieces by more cadavers. Another had been pinned against a wall and was being disembowelled by a SS guard he'd once stood alongside.

Dead ahead, Barton was doing everything he could to protect the prisoners whilst beating back more of the advancing undead.

Obersturmbannführer Scherler made his move.

As the area descended into chaos once more, he ran for cover, pushing Doctor Månsson ahead of him at gun point. In the confusion Månsson had let the little girl go. He screamed for her to follow him but she appeared catatonic. There was nothing any of them could do to stop her being swallowed up by the rotting hordes.

Wilkins knew what he had to do. 'Barton, get these innocent people to safety, then get to the rendezvous point and tell Captain Hunter I'm on my way. And hurry, we've barely any time!'

Barton did as he was ordered, ushering those prisoners still at hand back into the shack where they'd previously been held at gunpoint. He paused only to dispatch four more Nazis – three already dead, one who'd still been alive – before shutting the civilians inside and leaving them with as many guns as he could quickly lay his hands on. 'I don't know if you can understand a single word I'm saying, but stay here. We'll send help. You'll not be left here long.'

He closed the door and ran for the hole in the border fence as Wilkins had ordered.

POLONEZKÖY
FORTY MINUTES TO RENDEZVOUS

The Nazi's boots echoed off the walls of the castle tower. He'd used an entrance hitherto unseen, but the noise Obersturmbannführer Scherler made as he barked orders and abuse at Doctor Månsson left Wilkins in no doubt as to where he was heading.

Wilkins skidded around a corner to see the Nazi just ahead. He ducked back under cover as the German officer fired at him, one bullet hitting the wall above his head, showering him with dust and debris.

'There's no way out, Fritz,' Wilkins shouted, but the German was in no mood to capitulate.

'You are right. There's no way out for any of us, you British fool. We are all going to die here today.'

'I told you, it doesn't have to be this way.'

'I rather think it does.'

Scherler was heading upwards now, to the top of one of the towers either side of the castle entrance. Wilkins was exhausted and the thought of climbing again filled him with dread. Less than half an hour to go... it seemed that all was lost. What was the point?

Everything depends on what you do now, old boy, he told himself. *Everything!*

Wilkins began to ascend the spiral staircase, pressing himself flat against the wall as another ferocious volley of bullets was sent his way. As soon as they'd stopped he ran on, but he'd been lulled into a false sense of security and the German fired at him again, hitting his left shoulder. Wilkins screamed out in pain but kept moving for all he was worth. Just a flesh wound, but by God it hurt.

At the very top of the tower, weak with effort and soaked with sweat and blood, knowing his enemy could go no further from here, he readied himself to face the German. He emerged onto the flat roof of the tower, the highest part of the castle.

The doctor was on his knees with the Nazi's gun aimed at his head. When he saw Wilkins, Scherler aimed at him instead.

'Let the doctor go, and I'll let you go,' Wilkins said.

The German laughed. Nervous, slightly maniacal. 'Do you really believe you have any bargaining power? You British are so arrogant, so superior... and so predictable. You think you hold all the aces where, in fact, you hold none.'

'We'll all have been dealt a pretty awful hand if this infection isn't stopped, don't you think?'

'Not at all... with Doctor Månsson's help, the Fuhrer's plan to create the Aryan master-race will soon be complete.'

'Never,' Månsson spat, and he caught a vicious thump to the back of his head for his troubles. He slumped to the ground, unconscious.

'You bloody fool,' Wilkins sighed. 'He's our only hope. Don't you see that? Månsson can help us stop this germ in its tracks.'

'But we have no need to do that. Our beautiful disease must be allowed to flourish. Doctor Månsson has been working on a cure, a way of ensuring only those we want to survive will stay alive. A way of cleansing the planet like no other, leaving only the master race behind. Do you not yet realise you're beaten, you British pig?'

'And you think Månsson will help you?'

'You make it sound like he has a choice.'

'There's always a choice.'

Wilkins raised his pistol higher and aimed directly at the German's head. Scherler glared at him. 'I'll put a bullet in his brain if you take another step nearer. Now put down your weapon.'

And then a single shot rang out, echoing through the early morning gloom.

Wilkins checked himself for further injury, but there was none. The German staggered back, clutching his chest. But who had fired? Wilkins looked around and saw Steele on the top of the opposite tower, gesticulating wildly for his commanding officer to get moving.

But the Nazi wasn't finished yet.

With the last dregs of energy he could summon, he fired his rifle repeatedly at Doctor Månsson. The scientist's body twitched and jerked violently.

'You evil bastard!' Wilkins shouted, and he fired his weapon at the German again and again, each shot forcing him further and further back towards the battlements. 'Do you know what you've done? You've condemned the entire world to a fate worse than death.'

The Nazi grinned through blood-stained teeth. The sickening smile was too much for Wilkins to stand and he fired twice more, the final shot sending the kraut over the top of the tower's battlements. He fell like a stone, bouncing off the roof of another part of the castle below, then landing in a crumpled heap in the courtyard. Wilkins peered down after him. The dawn light was sufficient now for him to be able to make out every detail as hordes of the dead descended on the fatally wounded German officer.

Månsson lay shuddering on the cold ground, his life draining away with the blood that trickled down the spiral staircase. Wilkins crouched down and the doctor pulled him closer. He said something, but it was hard to make out. 'What are you saying, man?'

'The girl,' Månsson said, his voice little more than a drowned croak now as his lungs filled with blood. 'She's the one...'

'I don't understand. What girl?'

'She's the cure...'

'What girl?' he asked again, frantic now, but it was too late. Månsson was dead.

Steele appeared from the staircase. 'Come on, Lieutenant. We need to move. We've barely minutes left to get out of here.'

Wilkins knelt over the dead doctor. 'There's no point running, Steele. It's over. I fear our number's up.'

'Not quite,' he said. 'There's something you need to see.'

Steele had to drag Wilkins over to the side of the tower and force him to look down. At first all Wilkins could see was chaos. Vast numbers of the dead had escaped the confines of the concentration camp and were swarming out through the surrounding countryside, many of them heading for the airfield at Leginów where the sounds of distant action could be heard. Many more remained trapped in the camp itself, either unable to get out or still intent on hunting down the remaining few survivors. Another crowd had formed around the hut where the last few desperate prisoners of war continued to shelter.

And down there, right in the middle of the madness, was the small girl that Doctor Månsson had clung onto so desperately. She was easy to see, because the dead weren't attacking her. In fact, Wilkins realised, the foul things were positively avoiding her. A significant bubble of space had formed around her, and the space moved as she did.

Creatures backed out of her way, tripping over each other to move.

'It's incredible, isn't it, sir,' said Steele, 'she must somehow be immune.'

'Good Lord, you might be right. Whatever she is, she's our best chance,' Wilkins agreed. 'In fact, as far as I can see she's now our *only* chance. Come on, man!'

THE AIRFIELD
SEVENTEEN MINUTES TO RENDEZVOUS

Hunter's men had just about managed to hold the airfield. Border patrols picked off the few undead stragglers that had followed the earlier rancid crowds but had taken longer to get here. Despite a sudden flurry of activity when Polonezköy had been rocked by fresh explosions, the Americans remained unquestionably on top. They were just waiting on their ride out of here and, the captain hoped, for the return of Wilkins and his men with their precious passenger. And all of this had been done with barely a single shot being fired. Stealth and savagery had been the order of the day.

Bryce Hamilton, a battle-hardened warrior who'd seen more service than most, had been patrolling the outskirts of the forest near the far end of the airfield when he saw one of his colleagues go down unexpectedly. The man had been on his feet one minute, on the ground the next. He ran over to see what was wrong.

'Wassup, Wilder?'

Wilder was on his back, kicking out at something in the shadows. It was the remains of a Nazi that had hauled itself some distance to get here. Its legs were broken and useless, but it clearly still had enough brutal strength in its arms to move and was still completely fixated on destroying the living. It dragged itself further up Wilder's body, having completely taken him by surprise. Hamilton knocked off its helmet, grabbed a handful of hair, and pulled its head and neck up high enough so that Wilder could kick his way free. The creature, unable to support itself from the waist down, flipped over onto its back and, before it could react, Hamilton stamped on its face until it stopped thrashing and lay completely still.

'Thanks, man,' Wilder gasped, picking himself up and brushing himself down. 'Damn thing came outta nowhere.'

'Yeah, and it wasn't alone...'

Hamilton pushed past Wilder and struck another creature square in the face with the butt of his rifle. And another. Wilder was alongside him now, and they saw that more of the monsters were swarming through the trees, all moving in this direction.

'Where the hell are they coming from so suddenly?' Wilder asked, confused and concerned.

Hamilton didn't answer. He called for assistance and was relieved when he heard other members of the battalion moving towards them. He stared into the blood-soaked face of the next corpse he dispatched. Female? Although his view was limited in the low light, he realised the woman lying at his feet was dressed in the uniform of a prisoner. Had she come from Polonezköy? 'Wait,' he started to say, 'are these...?'

One of the vile creatures hurled itself at him at speed. He instinctively caught the cadaver and was about to smack the damn thing in its hideous face when it spoke.

'Wait, don't. It's me, Lance Corporal Barton. Get me to Captain Hunter. Urgently!'

The accent gave the man away. It was one of the Brits. Hamilton obliged, virtually dragging the British soldier back to the airfield, then pushing him up the makeshift runway.

It took a couple of minutes to reach the captain. Barton could barely breathe, let alone speak. By the time they got to him, though, the captain was already well aware there was a problem. A vast swarm of the dead was beginning to emerge from the tree-line, rapidly encroaching on the airfield. Their shadowy shapes were everywhere. Hunter could see his men trying to keep them at bay; to a man they were doing everything they could, beating the hell out of everything that moved, but numbers meant they were already being forced to retreat.

'Where's Lieutenant Wilkins and the doctor?' Hunter demanded, no time for pleasantries.

Barton shook his head and sucked in oxygen. 'Not yet... Message from the lieutenant... He says to wait... almost done...'

'We can't afford to wait, goddammit. And where the hell did all these spooks appear from?'

'The camp... the walls have been breached... Hundreds of them coming this way...'

'Does Wilkins have the doctor?'

'Not sure.'

'And I'm supposed to risk the lives of my remaining men on your uncertainty?'

'Lieutenant Wilkins won't let us down, sir.'

'Yeah, well it ain't just us who's in trouble, is it?'

Captain Hunter stormed away, barking orders at his men, moving them down from the top end of the airfield towards the trees to stem the ever-growing advance of the dead.

Someone asked an obvious question, and Hunter gave them an equally obvious reply, bellowing at the top of his voice. 'Do whatever you have to. Shoot the shit out of those bastards, just keep them off this damn runway. I want that Douglas to get a clear approach and to be able to get away again. I do *not* intend on being stranded in the middle of this shit-storm. Do I make myself clear?'

His troops' reply went unheard amongst the cacophony of gunfire which suddenly filled the air.

THE CAMP COURTYARD
THIRTEEN MINUTES TO RENDEZVOUS

The dead seemed to come at Wilkins and Steele like a tsunami of rotting flesh. 'No need for quiet anymore, eh Lieutenant?' Steele said, and he ran headlong into the crowd, firing shot after shot at the foul cadavers. It was impossible to spot the little girl in the madness out here, and equally impossible to stop and search for her.

'Split and find her,' Wilkins ordered, shouting after him. 'Holler when you have her. Remember the whole world depends on us.'

He too ran into the chaos, doing everything he could to ignore the searing pain in his left shoulder and still hold onto his pistol with his good right hand. He chose each shot with as much care as he could, knowing that once this round was spent, he wouldn't have time to reload.

Steele headed for the area where he thought he'd last seen the girl. There was just a forest of sickly cadavers here now, balancing on spindly legs, all of them pivoting awkwardly when they heard him, starting to move in his direction. He dove through them, battering some away with his rifle and shooting others, feeling like he was about to drown in this rotting tide.

And then he thought he saw her.

Nothing, just more bodies. Had he been mistaken?

He shot a foetid Nazi between the eyes, and when the hideous creature dropped, he saw clear space behind.

There she was!

He could see her intermittently between the ghouls which still surged towards him. They were coming at him with ever increasing speed and ferocity, not giving up and not letting him pass. One caught his jacket, another the strap of his rifle, a third clung onto his leg... but Steele kept moving because he could definitely see her now, almost touch her...

One last push...

He broke through and grabbed the girl's hand, and as soon as he had hold of her it was as if he had become invisible to the diseased masses. They turned away and he moved among them without fear. Impervious. And as for the girl beside him – she was the strangest creature. Pallid skin, ice-cold to the touch... anyone would think she was dead. It occurred to him that she most likely was, and it took all the inner strength he could muster not to let go of her tiny hand.

'I've got her, Lieutenant,' he shouted, but his voice was drowned out by the engines of the Douglas aircraft which swept down low over the camp on its way to the airfield.

Less than ten minutes remaining.

Captain Woody Rickman couldn't believe the chaos on the ground below him. 'You seeing this, Garfunkle?'

'Yeah, I see it,' his co-pilot replied.

From the air, Polonezköy looked like it was imploding. Palls of dirty grey smoke rose up from several unchecked fires. The guards had clearly lost control, because the prisoners were unrestrained. They were fighting with each other to get out through an ugly breach in the outer fence. And there were bodies everywhere; the grubby grey courtyard was awash with blood.

Rickman guided the Douglas out towards the airfield. On the ground below he could see a constant stream of prisoners making their way in the same direction they were heading. 'Jeez, they'd better have that landing strip clear, otherwise we ain't putting down.'

'It'll be clear. Captain Hunter's a good man. He'll have the job done.'

Rickman pointed down. 'It's not him I'm worried about, it's them. Even if we get down, chances are we're going to struggle to get back up again. What's the betting all those people are going to want a ride out of this place.'

'Well we ain't taking none of them,' Garfunkle said, indignant. 'Wasn't our brief.'

'I know that and you know that, Garfunkle, but try telling them.'

POLONEZKÖY
EIGHT MINUTES

Steele looked for Wilkins, and Wilkins looked for the girl. She had to be here somewhere, Wilkins thought, but he kept glancing over at the hole in the border fence, wondering if she'd managed to escape. His energy was flagging, and his feelings of abject loss and desolation were increasing by the second. In some ways it would have been easier to have missed by a mile. To have come so close to success yet to have still failed was tantamount to cruelty.

Did he run now and try to get away, or did he keep looking until the last possible second? Was there any point in running and heading home empty-handed? Would there even be a home left to run back to?

He'd fought with so many dead bodies since being back out in the open that it had almost become second nature, like working on a factory assembly line where one slip could mean infinitely more than losing your job. He tried to focus on re-killing as best he could while he continued to look for the girl.

Go for the head.

Knife first, then fist, then pistol.

Keep fighting.

Don't stop.

Don't think about the odds.

But as he gouged his blade through the eye of a blood-splattered, grey-skinned dead SS officer, Wilkins couldn't help but remember how heavily the odds were stacked against him now. He liked a flutter as much as the next man, but he wouldn't have bet so much as a penny on him getting out of this scrape alive.

Still more corpses. For every one which went down without a fight, several more came at him with real tenacity and venom. His arms felt like lead... how much longer?

Another wave. Deep breath.

Wilkins dug in and struck out again, cutting into the neck of another obnoxious ex-SS cadaver. He miss-timed and carved a jagged slice across the creature's neck, and when it slumped forward he was drenched in its foul-smelling rotten blood. The next one came at him and he stabbed at its face. His blade disappeared into its gaping maw, then sunk into the back of its throat. His hands still wet with blood, the handle of his clasp knife slipped from his grip and the ghoul tripped away with his knife still wedged between its jaws.

Just the pistol left now.

Only a handful of bullets.

He fired once, missing the brain but hitting the chest of another corpse. The impact of the shot was enough to send it spiralling away.

The next one was a perfect hit. Right between the eyes.

The next one was nowhere near as elegant, but he did enough damage to bring the vile thing down.

The next one wore the drab, blood-stained uniform of a prisoner. Particularly insistent, it managed to hook its gnarled fingers in the folds of his smock. Another caught his trousers. One crawling along the ground had his boot. Despite their slothful speed, he was in real danger of being overwhelmed. He tried to beat them off, but there were too many...

The next one was pointing a gun directly at him.

He froze. Panicked. Went to fire back but hesitated.

'Lieutenant Wilkins?'

Wilkins realised he must have looked an awful fright, covered in dirt and discharge from the undead as well as his own sweat and blood. He was surprised Steele had even recognised him. He'd have told him as much, but he barely had the energy to breathe, let alone talk. Steele kicked out at another cadaver as it went to attack the lieutenant. Wilkins raised his pistol to fire at one more, but the chamber clicked empty. 'I should have saved two bullets for us, Sergeant,' he gasped.

'Why, sir? I've no intention of falling at the last hurdle.'

And Wilkins realised that Steele was holding the hand of Doctor Månsson's precious little girl.

'Good Lord.'

'She'll help get us out of here, Lieutenant. Stay close to me.'

The numerous creatures which had, just seconds earlier, seemed intent on tearing the lieutenant limb from limb, were now doing everything in their limited power to get away from him or, more specifically, from Månsson's girl. They scampered away from her like the rats they'd earlier seen spilling out along the castle corridors.

'I think she's dead, Lieutenant, but she's not like the rest of them. She's different. She's the cure, I reckon. She seems to repel them like oil and water. It's like they're scared of her.'

'Then let's get her out of here and fast,' Wilkins said, his energy and composure beginning to return. 'She may well be mankind's last hope.'

The girl gave the soldiers a degree more freedom than they were used to. Wilkins was already heading for the gaping hole in the fence, readying himself to try and run to the airfield, but Steele called him back. 'Wait, Lieutenant.'

'Come on, man... the plane will be leaving any minute. We don't have time to delay.'

'We don't have time to get there, either.'

'Then what do you suggest?'

Carrying the girl over one shoulder like a sack of coal now, Steele pointed back into the camp with his free arm. A vehicle compound. Ignored by the rotting masses. 'Over there. Let's help ourselves to one of Jerry's supply trucks.'

THE AIRFIELD
FOUR MINUTES

Captain Hunter's men guided in the Douglas. Before the plane had even stopped moving, troops were surrounding it on all sides, firing into the trees. The dead were being called to the airfield in massive numbers. There had been thousands of them at Polonezköy, and since the fence there had been down, they'd almost exclusively been drawn in this direction. The surrounding countryside was deathly quiet in comparison to this place. Captain Hunter's men's on-going battle to secure the site had attracted large numbers, but nothing in comparison to the flood of decay that was heading here now from the camp. Until now Hunter had resisted allowing his men to use firearms, but the choice had been taken out of his hands. 'Hit them with everything you've got,' he bellowed across the battlefield. 'Wipe the damn things out.'

Barton was still struggling to catch his breath. His desperate sprint from the camp to here had been terrifying. 'Lieutentant Wilkins will be here, sir,' he said to the captain. 'I know he will.'

'We can't afford to wait, soldier.'

'We can't afford not to.'

'Maybe you don't understand me, boy, and maybe you do things differently round your neck of the woods, but way I see it we need to get this bird back up in the air in the next couple of minutes or none of us are gonna get out of here.'

'If the lieutenant's not with us, I don't think it matters, sir.'

Captain Hunter pretended not to hear. The ever-increasing noise of battle filled the air. Rickman had turned the Douglas around and was ready to open the throttle and get the hell out of Poland as soon as Hunter gave the word.

Barton yelled at the captain to understand, but got no response. He grabbed Hunter's arm and tried to plead with him, but all that did was incense the American even more. 'Get your hands off me, boy, and get your sorry ass on-board.'

'But, Captain...'

'Now, soldier! Get out of my sight or I'll leave you here to fight those damn freaks on your own. Your man's not coming back, and you just have to accept that. He tried, he failed. Now it's time, and we're leaving.'

Sergeant Prendergast, a kid who didn't look old enough to be in long trousers never mind the army, rushed up to the captain. 'We're gettin' swamped out there, Captain.'

Hunter nodded. He cast a look at Barton which told the British soldier in no uncertain terms that he needed to keep his mouth shut. Barton knew what was coming next.

'We're out of here,' Captain Hunter said. 'Get everyone on-board. Blow the shit out of the next line of corpses to stop any more getting through for a couple a minutes. We've waited here long enough.'

Prendergast nodded then sprinted back to the front line. Barton dejectedly boarded the plane. He looked back as a volley of grenades was launched into the forest. The tree-line exploded into flame. If Wilkins and Steele were caught up in the middle of all that, he thought, then between the explosions and the dead they didn't stand a cat in hell's chance of getting out of there alive.

But right now they were still fighting.

Steele sat next to Wilkins, cradling the grey-skinned, undead girl in his arms. Wilkins had taken an empty truck from the Nazi compound and had driven it out through the hole in the fence around Polonezköy at breakneck speed. At first, he'd tried driving around the swarming dead, but it had quickly become clear that such consideration was frivolous and unnecessary in the extreme. Instead he now drove through them, keeping his foot down hard on the accelerator, trying to focus on what was happening directly ahead and not be distracted by the thud-thud-thud of dead flesh on metal. Heads popped like balloons. Limbs were dragged under grinding wheels. Wilkins left the wipers on, but all they did was smear blood and decay in a greasy arc across the windscreen, obstructing his field of view.

'Straight, Lieutenant, straight!' Steele yelled as Wilkins yanked the wheel hard right.

'I can't risk driving through the forest,' Wilkins shouted back, jumping up in his seat as they drove over a particularly obese corpse then through an ice-covered pothole. 'I'm going to drive up and around the side of Polonezköy, then try and pick up a track near the entrance. There has to be a road from the camp to Leginów, don't you think?'

'You're probably right, but I don't reckon we've got time. We have to take the most direct route.'

'And if we do that, Sergeant, I don't think we'll ever get through.'

Another volley of grenades. The next wave of corpses, crawling frantically over the remains of the last, were blown to pieces. In places the gore was inches deep.

But still they came.

As dawn's light broke, the full horror of the scene was revealed. The dense forest between Polonezköy and the airfield was rife with teeming movement, the noise of battle having drawn almost every undead creature from the camp in this direction. Sure, the grenades and the gunfire would beat another load of them back, but it was clear there'd immediately be more to take their place. Captain Hunter reckoned there were far more attacking bodies than he had grenades for. 'We've done enough, men,' he told his sergeants. 'We're outta here.'

Hunter headed for the Douglas and disappeared inside, pausing on the step to look back once more. Much of the tree-line was ablaze, dirty smoke billowing into the sky. Soldiers still took pot-shots through the haze as they retreated, bringing down body after body after body. Almost as soon as the last man had stopped firing, the dead advanced again. And this time, with no suppressing fire to stop them, they made progress with terrifying speed. Less than a minute after the final shot had been fired and they'd already gained more than twenty yards ground from the trees. There was nothing left to hold them back. Clambering over the devastated husks of their fallen brethren, hundreds more of the dead spilled onto the airfield like an unstoppable slick.

Barton tried one last time to persuade Captain Hunter, but the American was having none of it. 'Please, sir, just a minute longer.'

'Lieutenant Wilkins is gone, son. He failed. Accept it.'

'But, sir...'

'Get this kid out of my face,' Hunter bellowed. He turned and shouted to the pilot. 'Captain Rickman, get us out of here.'

**

Wilkins' intuition had served him well. After racing along the western edge of the concentration camp, they eventually hit the gravel track which connected the camp to the airfield at Leginów. He kept his foot down on the pedal, trying to wring every last scrap of speed out of a tired old vehicle that was less racehorse, more packhorse.

Steele clung onto their precious cargo. 'Think we're going to do this?'

Wilkins' silence was as good an answer as he was going to get. Steele understood. He didn't think they were going to make it either.

Over a rise, through a water-filled dip, up another grinding climb, and they were almost there. Wilkins glanced across to his left. They were driving parallel with the airfield landing strip. He could see the Douglas' tail fin between the trees. Damn thing was moving!

'Hold on, Steele.'

'I am holding on. I've been holding on since we got into this damn jalopy.'

'Then you may need to hold a little tighter.'

Without warning, Wilkins steered hard left, almost tipping the truck over onto its side. A fortuitous glancing blow against a tree knocked the vehicle back down onto all four wheels and Wilkins accelerated again. The truck crashed through the undergrowth, bringing down saplings and bushes, and weaving between more established trees, then smashed through a wire-mesh fence which ran alongside the runway. They emerged perhaps two hundred yards ahead of the Douglas, which was already taxiing down the bumpy strip, ready to take off.

'He'll never stop now,' Steele said.

'Don't worry. I'll make him see us.'

And for the second time in a minute, Wilkins steered hard left. The truck turned in a wide arc, facing back down the runway, and he accelerated again.

Wilkins was driving headlong at the Douglas. And behind the aircraft, hundreds of crazed bodies raced towards them.

'What the hell is that idiot doing?' Garfunkle asked. 'Damn Nazis. Do they think we're gonna give them a lift home or something?'

'We'll keep going,' Captain Rickman told him. 'Fly right over that crazy fool and let him run straight into that lot following behind us. Serve the damn kraut right.'

Garfunkle kept the throttle open, trying to work out if they had enough space to get up off the ground and clear the truck. He thought they'd make it. Just.

'Wait...' Rickman said. 'Is that...?'

He'd recognised Wilkins and Steele at the last possible second and slowed the plane down. Captain Hunter was up with the pilots almost instantly. 'What the hell? Get us out of here, for Christ's sake.'

'It's the Brits, sir, look,' said Garfunkle.

'God damn,' the captain cursed before turning to shout an order to the troops out back. 'Get them on-board, and quick. Wait any longer and we'll never get off the ground.' He turned back to Rickman and Garfunkle. 'How much space do you fellas need to get us up in the air?'

'A little more than we've got,' Rickman answered.

They'd seen them, they must have. Wilkins thought his eyes were deceiving him at first but no, the Douglas had definitely stopped on the runway. He accelerated again until they were level with the plane, then steered right and made sure he stopped more than a wing's width away. 'Come on, Sergeant, let's go home.'

Steele hoisted the child onto his shoulder again and began to run alongside Wilkins, but both of them stopped when they saw the size of the crowd of foetid corpses coming their way from the direction of Polonezköy. It looked enormous. So many that they both knew beyond doubt there was a real chance the plane could be surrounded by dead flesh in the next couple of minutes.

The hatch in the side of the Douglas opened. Barton was there with a couple of yanks, beckoning them to move. 'Lieutenant Wilkins! Quick!' he screamed.

'As if that hadn't occurred to me,' Wilkins muttered under his breath. He pushed Steele forward first, and Steele offered the girl to the first soldier who reached down. Captain Hunter pushed himself between the soldier and Steele.

'What the hell is that thing?' he demanded. 'You ain't bringing one of those damn creatures on this aircraft.'

'All due respect, Captain,' Wilkins explained, 'this girl will probably save more lives than you and I and our respective companies put together. There's no time to explain. Please trust me.'

Hunter reluctantly moved aside, and Steele and Wilkins boarded the Douglas. 'Let's get outta here,' the captain shouted, and the plane immediately began to lurch forward again. Wilkins was still half-in and half-out, hanging back. He could see the dead getting perilously close behind. Some of them were in touching distance now. Some had their decaying hands on the plane's fuselage and were attempting to work their way towards the wings. Two Americans pulled the door shut and he dropped down into the nearest available seat and strapped in. He craned his neck to look back.

The dead were still running after them. It was like something out of a nightmare. Would they never stop?

Captain Rickman opened the throttle fully and pulled back on the controls. The plane bounced along the uneven grass, rapidly running out of airstrip. He glanced across at Garfunkle and saw his co-pilot had his eyes screwed shut.

The Douglas lifted off the ground, its landing gear clipping the trees as it climbed into the air.

Wilkins kept looking down, watching the bodies below them disappear. Polonezköy looked impossibly bleak in the cold light of morning, like a scab on the face of the planet. Poisoned. Overrun by the dead.

Was this to be the fate of the entire world?

Or had he and his men done enough?

AT THE FRONT
TO THE WEST – NAMUR

Private Fred McCarthy took aim from the hayloft hideout where he'd spent what felt like forever since the dead had attacked. He fired, felling another one of the foul monsters, then put down his weapon and scratched another mark on the wooden window frame. Sixty-eight in total.

Gunfire came sporadically from the farmhouse across the way, but McCarthy reckoned only one or two of the boys were left fighting now. Most others were gone. He hoped they'd got the hell out of here, but he knew they probably hadn't. He thought it most likely that they were undead now; damned to keep fighting and keep killing until their decaying bodies failed them.

McCarthy had only a couple of shots left. He thought he should make them count, but he knew it didn't really matter. A few more of them taken out would barely make any difference now when so many remained. The one he'd just brought down had been already replaced by many more, and as the sun rose and cast long, dragging shadows towards the village of Namur, he saw that there were hundreds still coming across the fields.

The ground floor of the barn was full of dead flesh. The place was surrounded, too. McCarthy couldn't see a way out. And they knew he was up here, he was sure they did. He'd heard them on the steps, and one of them was hammering at the hatch trying to get to him now. It wouldn't be long before they got inside. They'd keep coming until their sheer combined bulk forced the hatch open.

He slumped in the corner with his back against the wall and waited for the inevitable. It was just a few minutes later when the wood splintered and they came surging up into the loft.

McCarthy saved a bullet for the first of them, but wished he'd held onto it for the creature following immediately behind. Sergeant Phillips. The reanimated corpse of his squad leader was trapped halfway through the hatch. McCarthy had a single bullet left. Did he put his sergeant out of his eternal misery, or end his own suffering before it began?

The shot rang around the flesh-filled farm, echoing across the emptiness, causing the dead to surge and herd again, converging on the isolated outpost. McCarthy lowered himself out of the hayloft window and dropped into the decaying crowd below, using them to cushion his fall.

He was up and on his feet again in seconds. Punching and shoving with one hand, slicing and stabbing with the blade he held in the other. From here it looked like all of mainland Europe had been overcome by the dead, but McCarthy was still alive, and by God, he was going to go out fighting.

AT THE FRONT
TO THE EAST – THE
ELSENBORN RIDGE

The shells were fired as quickly as they could be delivered to the front. In the space of a couple of days, the entire area had been all but destroyed, changed beyond all recognition. Virtually no tree remained standing in the Rocherath forest. Craters were filled with ice- and snow-covered bodies. For as far as anyone could see in any direction, human remains covered the ground.

But still they kept fighting.

The decaying enemy continued to advance, their numbers undiminished, but the 99th Infantry Division would never surrender.

AT THE FRONT
SOUTH OF BASTOGNE

They'd spent too long on the back-foot. It was time to reverse the tide.

Lieutenant Coley ordered a group of men to advance onto a section of land that had just been hit with a barrage of shells. 'Get in quick,' he shouted over the chaos. 'You find anything moving out there, you hit it hard until it lies still. Understand?'

'Yessir,' came the reply from several American soldiers as they piled forward.

Coley felt a hard slap on his shoulder and he span around fast, rifle primed and ready to fire. 'Whoa, now, take it easy,' said Escobedo. 'Good to see you too, Lieutenant.'

'Sorry, Escobedo. Never been so tired, but I've never been so keen to keep fighting, neither.'

'I know what you mean.'

'Can't remember the last time I slept for anything longer than a couple of minutes.'

'You making progress here, though?'

'It's damn slow, but yeah. We're getting there. We're moving in the right direction now, at least.

Tactics are pretty straightforward – hit 'em hard, then clear the way through.'

Escobedo went to move on, but then stopped. He checked himself. Munitions exploded in the near distance, and a prolonged barrage of machine gun fire ripped through the air nearby. Foul-smelling smoke drifted between the two men. 'Reckon we're going to make it?' he asked.

'Damn right we are, soldier,' Coley said without hesitation. 'There's no way we're going to let all this have been for nothing. Get your head down, get fighting, and keep fighting 'til there's not a single one of those diseased bastards left standing. You hear me?'

'I hear you, sir,' Escobedo said, and he shouldered his rifle and charged headlong into battle.

Coley surveyed the devastation ahead of him. A world in ruins. Americans killing Americans who'd already died once before. Nazis fighting alongside sworn enemies to defeat an even greater foe. Civilians burning corpses and delivering supplies.

This was a battle which had to be fought.

A war which had to be won.

POCKLINGTON HALL

Wilkins barely had time to get himself clean and his wounds seen to before he found himself in front of Colonel Adams again. 'Good job, Wilkins,' the colonel said. 'It appears that strange little girl you brought back with you might just be the key. Our scientists believe she carries enough information to enable them to understand this abhorrent condition and put an end to it. She's infected with a variant of the germ, by all accounts.'

'Doctor Månsson gave his life to protect her.'

'Then let us hope his sacrifice wasn't in vain.'

The colonel seemed downbeat. Broken, almost. Wilkins tried to focus but all he wanted was to go out into the operations room and look for Jocelyn. He thought he'd caught a glimpse of her through a window a few moments ago. There'd been times in the last few hours he'd thought he'd never see her again.

'The news from the front isn't good, Wilkins. The situation is at tipping point. Between the Nazis and the undead, our forces are being beaten back. We're struggling to hold ground.'

'So the sooner our chaps can produce a cure, the better.'

'If only it were that simple. As quickly as we're trying to tame the disease, the Nazis are doing everything they can to increase and harness its power, to rid themselves of its unpredictability. By all accounts, we understand they're close to cracking the problem too.'

The news was like a hammer blow to Wilkins. 'Good Lord. What can we do?'

'We believe an all-out assault on the bunker in Berlin where the work is being carried out is the only option available to us.'

'A bunker? In the German capital? The very heart of the Reich's stranglehold on power? Such a mission would be suicidal.'

Colonel Adams gestured for Wilkins to follow him. 'Come with me.'

He took Wilkins down into the bowels of Pocklington Hall again, past the guarded door to the room where the undead remains of Raymond Mills continued to be held (and Wilkins could hear Mills crashing about in there even now). They came to another door in another corridor, guarded by two imperious-looking, black-suited troops. They exchanged salutes, then the colonel waved them away. Working in perfect synchronisation, the guards both turned keys in the door then slid across bolts and released latches.

It was more like the door to a bank vault than a prison cell, and inside it looked more like a hotel room than a gaol.

The relatively luxurious looking room had a single occupant. SS- Obergruppenführer Jakob Wolfensohn stood to attention, clicked his heels and saluted.

'It appears we have a way in,' Colonel Adams said.

TOGETHER AT LAST...
BUT FOR HOW LONG?

Wilkins held Jocelyn tight as they watched the golden sun dip below the horizon. The grounds of Pocklington Hall were silent, as if every last man and woman were resting in preparation for the next fight. 'Promise you'll never leave me again?' she whispered.

Wilkins looked deep into her beautifully clear eyes. He pictured them becoming clouded with infection. He pictured Jocelyn's perfect lips drawing into a snarl and her teeth biting into his flesh. He pictured his wonderful fiancé transformed into one of those hellish creatures he'd fought in Bastogne and at Polonezköy, damned to walk the Earth in endless pain for all eternity.

'No, my love, I cannot make such a promise.'

'But you must.'

'Not until the war is won, Jocelyn. Not until the world is rid of both the Nazis and the undead menace they have unleashed.'

'But Robert, you've done your part.'

'No, Jocelyn. My fight has only just begun.'

AFTERWORD

I was honoured to be asked to be a part of this project by Craig and Tim, who'd come up with the idea for the series in May 2015 while they'd been discussing the zombie genre at Crypticon Seattle. When the invitation came I said yes without hesitation.

Those of you who know my work will also know that this book is very different to the usual kind of story I write. My books are usually contemporary in their setting, and almost always feature a cast of ordinary people who find themselves thrust, usually through no fault of their own, into extraordinary situations. Wrong place, wrong time.

When I started researching and writing this book, it struck me how many millions of people found themselves in that exact situation during World War II: ordinary people, extraordinary situations. Sitting here now, enjoying a life of relative comfort and security, it's easy to forget that, not too long ago, untold numbers of men and women were forced to make the ultimate sacrifice to protect our freedoms. As time goes on and we increasingly focus on the many issues of today, we can lose sight of the efforts and achievements of those just a few generations older than ourselves.

Writing this book brought a lot of things into focus for me. It left me with a new found appreciation and respect for those who lived and served through World War II.

I'm no history scholar or military buff, so I have taken numerous massive liberties with the facts (we're writing about zombies after all!). Though the events of the Battle of the Bulge form a backdrop to this novel and to the entire series, the further we get from Tim's excellent first novel, the more fantastic our story will inevitably become. This book is an adventure story at heart, one which might have been torn from the pages of a tattered copy of Boy's Own back in the day, and I very much hope that you've enjoyed it.

I can't wait to see what Craig has in store for us in BERLIN OR BUST!

ABOUT THE AUTHORS

DAVID MOODY grew up on a diet of trashy horror and pulp science fiction. He worked as a bank manager before giving up the day job to write about the end of the world for a living.

He has written a number of horror novels, including AUTUMN, which has been downloaded more than half a million times since publication in 2001 and spawned a series of sequels and a movie starring Dexter Fletcher and David Carradine.

Film rights to HATER were snapped up by Guillermo del Toro (Hellboy, Pan's Labyrinth, Pacific Rim) and Mark Johnson (Breaking Bad). Moody lives with his wife and a houseful of daughters and stepdaughters, which may explain his preoccupation with Armageddon. Find out more about Moody:

www.davidmoody.net
www.infectedbooks.co.uk

ABOUT THE AUTHORS

CRAIG DILOUIE is the author of SUFFER THE CHILDREN (Simon & Schuster, May 2014) and the bestselling zombie novels TOOTH AND NAIL (START/Salvo Press, April 2010), THE INFECTION (Permuted Press, February 2011), its sequel THE KILLING FLOOR (Permuted Press, April 2012), and the RETREAT series with Joe McKinney and Stephen Knight.

He has also authored the CRASH DIVE series, a WWII submarine thriller; THE GREAT PLANET ROBBERY, a military sci-fi comedy; and PARANOIA, a psychological thriller.

As a technical writer, he has also written several non-fiction books about lighting and electrical design.

Craig blogs about apocalyptic and horror books and films regularly at:

www.craigdilouie.com

ABOUT THE AUTHORS

TIMOTHY W LONG has been writing tales and stories since he could hold a crayon and has read enough books to choke a landfill. Tim has a fascination with all things zombie, a predilection for weird literature, and a deep-seated need to jot words on paper and thrust them at people. Tim spent time in the US Navy, worked for a major game corporation, an aeronautics company, and he has been in the IT field for the last 15 years as an engineer before becoming a full time author. He is an active member of Horror Writers Association, SFWA, and International Thriller Writers.

Tim resides outside of Seattle where he spends time with his partner in crime, Amanda, as well as 2 children, 2 dogs of various sizes and dispositions, and a near constant supply of overpriced and overcooked coffee beans.

http://timothywlong.com

Printed in Great Britain
by Amazon

18421281R00164